TIME TRAVEL

+

BRAIN STEALING

=

MURDEROUS APPLIANCES AND GOOD TIMES

By

Richard Steele

TENTH STREET PRESS

THIS EDITION

© Copyright 2019 Richard Steele
Published by Tenth Street Press 2019
Cover design by Axel for Tenth Street Press

ISBN-10: 0-6484802-1-6
ISBN-13: 978-0-6484802-1-1

Also available as digital books

ISBN-10: 0-6484802-0-8
ISBN-13: 978-0-6484802-0-4

TENTH STREET PRESS
MELBOURNE   SEATTLE   LONDON
www.tenthstreetpress.com
Email: contact@tenthstreetpress.com

To my sons,
May you never read this book and if you do,
Dad's sorry

To my wife,
The fact you read this and we're not divorced means
I'm either a very lucky man,
Or I'm about to be smothered in my sleep

CONTENTS

PREFACE

Think you know your sci-fi horror genre like the back of your hand? Well prepare to have the back of your hand surgically removed and replaced with a chocolate chip pancake, forcing you to decide between a functional appendage and the very food necessary to survive, whilst you dangle trapped in a cage hung over a pit full of man-eating synonyms.

That's what this book has in store for you. A lot of bad choices, cliché moments, terribly scripted villains and nonsensical violence.

Things are going to get stranger than having your sister accidently kiss you at a county fair kissing booth, only for her to line up for seconds.

I will be here with you every step of the way, an omnipresent narrator with the tools to keep you on course, give you a hint or two, and berate the main characters for your enjoyment. Your instincts must be like a fart after an all you can eat Indian curry buffet. Don't trust them.

Follow these rules, throw your brain out the door and enjoy the read.

PART I
THE DUMPSTER OF DOOM

Chapter One
It Has Begun

It was a dull, dreary, desolate day in the humble town of Doomsville. It is a small town full of dejected, demoralized and despondent people living day to day, drudging through their dismal lives. Unbeknown to the dishevelled and doleful masses were the plans of a deceitful and deranged Doctor of Doom waiting in the shadows, diligently toiling away at his despicable master plan to enshroud Doomsville in a permanent prism of dread.

This unknown Professor of Pain with a predilection for punishment, has perfected his primary ability of converting inanimate objects into precise predators to prey on the population. Preposterous as it may seem, the plans made by this Practitioner of Panic have now been let loose on this sleepy town. Peace now stands as much chance as Peter Piper picking a peck of pickled peppers...or so he thought.

•

Waking from his dreamless sleep, Joe Brown stretched his extremities until he felt his bones pop and clambered out of his dilapidated single bed.

Looking across his jail sized room, Joe caught a glimpse of the time from his retro Casio watch, with built in calculator might I add.

7:55am, Saturday.

Joe dived head first into a mountain of dirty laundry piled up near his bedroom door, searching for that one pair of clean pants he knew were there. Rotting food, mice faeces and cockroach larvae were sporadically sprinkled amongst the one tonne heap as if they were toppings on a caramel sundae of filth.

'Victory!', he exclaimed, holding up a crusty set of blue jeans that pointed upwards like a perverted Excalibur pulled from a mythical rubbish tip rock.

Three days earlier, Joe's biological parents died in a cliché yet comical way that holds no importance to this story, forcing Joe to move in with his only living relative, his Godmother Aileen White. The unfortunate incident that claimed his parent's lives also destroyed his family home and all his belongings. Joe was left with only his deceased Godfather's room and clothes for comfort.

Aileen did the best she could while living on a disability pension due to a freak accident involving a pair of chopsticks and a llama. However, it was barely enough to provide for the growing fifteen-year-old boy that now lived above her in their squashed two-bedroom townhouse.

Did I mention that Joe's biological parents died in a cliché yet comical way that holds no importance to this story? Good, just checking.

Did I also mention Joe's house was now locked down under a large but completely irrelevant biohazard dome? Forget I mentioned it.

A voice echoed from downstairs.

"Breakfast is ready Joe."

Joe raced down the spiral staircase smelling what he believed to be a glorious breakfast of bacon and eggs awaiting him, only to find a singular piece of bacon hanging from a wire, attached to the ceiling fan. It was spinning like… a piece of bacon hanging from a wire attached to a ceiling fan, what did you expect?

"What! Not again Aileen, this isn't fair", pleaded Joe, for he had been 'baconned' again. Ever since the great bacon prank of 2015 he swore to himself it wouldn't happen again. But here he was, salivating like a ravenous cannibalistic female praying mantis after mating, only to find a bowl of sludge in its place.

"You know we are on a tight budget little man", Aileen screeched with a wisp of Irish youth in her frail old voice, "You'll just have to make do with my family's world-famous beef and squid eye porridge. Lots of protein for your growing muscles!"

Joe knew there was no beef in the porridge as he drove his jaw down on a chunk of rubbery squid eye, popping it open like a sour gelatinous egg filled with pus. The closest thing he had eaten to beef over the past three days was a can of Doomsville's finest home brand cat mince.

Joe knew better than to push the matter further with Aileen. She may be nearing sixty-three years old and have a spine so curved she could see yesterday, but with one flick of that tea towel she keeps tucked in her armpit high pants and she would turn Joe into a Julia very quickly.

Aileen held a dripping black garbage bag out for Joe which was two evolutionary steps away from forming its own consciousness. "And when you're done there Joey my boy, put this rubbish bag in the dumpster would you dear?"

"Ughh", sighed Joe, snapping out of his daydream about his parents and pushing it to the back of his mind once again.

"Yeah alright, but then I'm out of here for the day", Joe stated as firmly as he could, while at the same time protecting his privates from a tea towel rapture just in case. Sure, he would lose a finger or two, but it was a price he was willing to pay.

Aileen raised a suspicious brow so high that it migrated from her face and became a citizen of her ever-growing back hair, "Ok, you have a deal. But only because it's the weekend, and I don't want you moping around the house feeling sorry for yourself. Your parents wouldn't want that!" Extending her reptilian shaped hand in Joe's direction with all five fingers facing in ten different directions, he knew exactly what this meant for him.

The crusty kiss of death!

Her stained hand appeared unwashed since birth, with warts growing on warts creating a porous honeycomb of viral paradise for dirt and grime to bathe in. Hair attached to several moles across her palm were so long they were platted together in dreadlocks, and her skin was riddled with pustules that had reservoirs of oil deep enough to run a small car.

'Enough of the pleasantries', Joe told himself, building the courage to do what needed to be done.

Joe puckered his squid lips together and closed his eyes tighter than a squirrel grasping its last nut. Leaning forward he felt his lips break ground with Aileen's alien hand, surface craters and all. He lingered for a second. Any less and Aileen's other, even more disfigured hand would replace it for round two.

Appearing satisfied that Joe had met her disturbing ritualistic expectations, Aileen raised her chin upwards in an approving gesture. Although from Joe's perspective, standing at least six inches above this five-foot dwarf of a woman, it looked more like a one-hundred-year-old turtle with a misaligned jaw trying to lick its own nose.

Wasting no time, Joe snatched the top of the garbage bag and raced out the front door onto a concrete slab they called a front yard, narrowly avoiding six of Aileen's fifteen inbred cats. All the houses in Doomsville looked alike, the government officials thought it would promote uniformity, or so they said. Aileen's house was on a long, winding, narrow road aptly named Dooms Street with dozens of grey and white townhouses crammed together, ending in an abrupt cul-de-sac facing the local rubbish dump.

'Ahh, smell the serenity', Joe thought to himself as he shoulder-barged their aging iron gate open, sending a fresh layer of rusty mist high in the air.

Out on the verge was one of Doomsville's finest inventions. The self-closing, steel reinforced dumpster that compacted all your rubbish automatically, reducing the garbage collection to once a month. No one knew who came up with this great invention, only that he was a dark and mysterious man who clearly had the best intentions for the people of Doomsville and nothing else untoward.

"Piece of junk!", Joe yelled at the dumpster in frustration, kicking the side hatch button to prompt the lid to open.

Each dumpster had a unique code so that its contents could be read back at the rubbish dump to determine which sneaky individuals were breaching the forbidden 'No Human Waste' rule. Sounds like a no brainer? That's why there are toilets right? Unfortunately for Joe and Aileen, there were the occasional plumbing issues resulting in a few suspicious and smelly packages making their way into their dumpster.

To circumvent this issue, Joe used his superior intellect and even finer kicking abilities to knock a few wires loose in the dumpster's main processor and Presto! The dumpster is now their very own glorified toilet without the plumbing expense. Patent pending, so don't get any ideas!

As the dumpsters black domed lid slowly slid back like an armadillo unfurling, Joe stepped back and held the bin bag under his right arm with his legs bent and bottom sticking out. The green light on the side of the dumpster flashed indicating it was ready to receive.

'And receive it shall', thought Joe with a malice intent. He could never put a finger on why he hated this dumpster so much, only that it felt very primal, like a vegan who can hear the screams of a carrot as it's pulled from the ground. Think about that the next time you walk down the valley of death at your local grocery store you monster!

Sprinting with more co-ordination than an epileptic seal, Joe rushed at the dumpster and jumped as high as his teenage chicken legs could muster. Grabbing the bag from under his right arm, he mistimed his approach and slammed the bag on the bottom lip of the dumpster, sending human faeces' high into the air and coating their once black gate a new shade of brown.

"Ah shit", said Joe. And he was exactly right.

Using a nearby snot filled tissue, which was clearly Aileen's due to the amount of nose hair caught in it, Joe made a small gesture to clean up the crap-tashtrophe, wiping down the side of the dumpster so that its code could still be seen. If the code wasn't visible it wouldn't be picked up by the scanners on the rubbish trucks.

"Let's see, 3. V. 1. L. All there", Joe smiled at his brown reflection, happy with himself for completing the bare minimum in order to get back to his prearranged day.

What kind of day you ask? Only the best day Doomsville can offer. Firstly, a meetup with his best friend Brandon Red at the beach to observe the pod of dead whale carcasses that just recently washed ashore. Then, off to the central park of Doomsville for its annual 'Eat till you puke' contest, with special guest and world record bull testicle eater, Reginald Black. To finish this perfect day, Joe has a mid-afternoon cinema date with his high school crush Roxanne Beige, to watch the cult classic horror film, 'Chickens: A peck too far'.

Joe was so excited that in his haste he forgot his backpack with a change of clothes for his date with Roxanne. Looking down at his oversized T-shirt from his departed Godfather, which fit more like a dress over his child like body, Joe knew he needed something with a little more pizazz to win over Roxanne.

Running back through the front door and up the spiral staircase, Joe could hear Aileen outside his bedroom window screeching curse words he never knew existed.

"You're a lazy scoundrel Joe, I guess I'll clean up after you again! Wait till you feel the wrath of my tea towel tonight!"

Joe peeked out his bedroom window and saw Aileen hunched over in front of the dumpster, picking up what look like large brown logs of…

"Crap! Sorry Aileen", yelled Joe out the window, "I'm in a rush. I'll make it up to you I prom…argggghhh!"

Joe let out a scream. A long, high pitched, ear piercing, brain scrambling, glass shattering, testicle raising scream that was enough to send his puberty backwards a few years. Like watching a bad television commercial at midnight, Joe wanted to look away, but his eyes betrayed him, acting as his captors and forcing him to watch.

The cold black dumpster etched forward towards Aileen with its domed lid wide open, two red lights on either side of its lid acted like eyes, and out from its sides came two long grey metal arms with clamped prongs at each end. Aileen's small frame was nothing compared to the robust two-meter-wide and two-meter-tall dumpster, stooping over her like a diabetic craving a cupcake. Aileen had no time to make a noise as the dumpster grabbed her by her face and leg, throwing her three meters up in the air before she fell back down into the middle of the open lid.

Without hesitation, Joe tore down the stairs and picked up a crowbar near the front door before running outside. It was worse than he thought. More horrible than he could imagine. A lot gorier than he could dream of. And it all unfolded before his very eyes.

The dumpster's lid crushed down repeatedly onto Aileen's petite body, breaking her fragile torso apart into smaller and smaller pieces. Joe tried to hold back the tears as he wiped her spleen from his face. Breaking free from the full body paralysis he had been under, Joe grabbed the crowbar and forced it in-between the lid of the dumpster and the bottom lip, preventing it from shutting entirely.

Looking deep inside the dumpster, Joe could see Aileen's face, or at least he thought it was her face, it could have been the left overs of the beef and squid eye porridge, he wasn't sure. All he was sure of, was that the beef and squid eye porridge spoke to him. It said, "Joe.... your parents.... they didn't die...in a cliché...and unimportant way..."

Before Joe could reply, the crowbar bent in half under the pressure, closing the lid permanently where the dumpster began its compactification. Joe was defeated. He slumped down and leant against the gate watching the dumpster churn away, breaking bones and mixing organs. He was in shock.

'What happened? Did I do this? I ruined its processor...maybe it couldn't tell the difference between Aileen and garbage'. Joe ran the scenario through his mind, guilt building up in his conscience as his tears streamed down his blood covered face.

As if the heavens above, or in this case the hell below were listening, the dumpster suddenly stopped digesting and in slow motion reared its domed head to look directly at Joe. Joe swatted the side hatch button with a nearby stick to shut it down, but it had no effect. Its beady red eyes stared straight into Joes beady black eyes. Joe's stomach rumbled. The dumpster's body rattled. Joe let out a nervous fart. The dumpster emitted a cloud of smoke from its exhaust pipe. Joe realized his wasn't a fart.

Pulling soiled underpants out of his rear, Joe flexed all the muscles he could muster in an instinctual alpha male show of strength. Unfortunately for Joe, he looked more like a hairless cat straining to defecate in its litter box. The dumpster let out a loud booming laugh that echoed through the street. Joe looked up and down the road, but no-one was around. All the doors were closed and windows shut. It was a ghost town.

"I MUST FINISH WHAT MY MASTER MADE ME FOR", bellowed the dumpster in a deep robotic voice.

"What do you want from me?", Joe shouted back, his voice quivering as every bone in his body shook violently.

"YOUR...BRAIN!" it replied, with a hint of delight in its tone.

Once again, Joe's body betrayed him as his legs locked together refusing to part, preventing him from running. The dumpster crept forward on its squeaky plastic wheels.

'Surely a technologically advanced killing machine would have better wheels?', Joe thought as it gained distance on him, ten slow centimetres at a time. Joe closed his eyes and surrendered to the beast, having no will left to flee or fight.

Just as the dumpster extended its arms to clamp down on Joes unscathed face, another noise rang out in the distance causing the dumpster to stop in its tracks. It was the most majestic noise Joe had heard all day. The rubbish truck was coming.

The dumpster retracted its arms and spun around as it engaged its engine to maximum output, blasting away down the road towards the end of the cul-de-sac and into the rubbish dump.

Exhausted, Joe collapsed into a heap on the ground as his world turned to black.

•

Chapter Two
It Will Continue

"Hey boy! Wake up. Time to get going."

Fluttering his eyes and clearing the fog from his vision, Joe thought to himself, 'Was this all just a bad dream?' Placing both hands in front of his eyes as the fog cleared, Joe watched his pale pink hands turn a darker shade of red. Blood.

Looking around, Joe could see he was inside a holding cell at the local Doomsville Police station. It was a small two-manned station in the heart of the town, directly opposite the Doomsville Central Park.

The town was circular by nature. A layout designed by the local government to create a peaceful environment with its spiral layout, and in no way resembled a satanic pentagram.

A man of small stature was seated behind a desk, watching Joe intently. Joe recognized him as a deputy Sherriff by the looks of the silver shield on his chest. The man wore pitch black sunglasses that amplified his suspiciously long dark beard and had a thick red scar running from his left eye down to his jaw.

'Sunglasses inside?' Joe thought, 'And why does that beard look fake?'

Joe's eyes lingered on what appeared to be strings connected to the man's beard, all the while conspiracies about bearded circus women flooded his mind. Unable to grasp onto reality, Joe began to feel light headed again.

"Come on boy, get up now", the man said gruffly, still seated at his desk.

Joe slowly sat upright from his prone position and looked down. He had a change of clothes on him, the kind given to suspects who have their clothes seized for evidence, leaving Joe looking like a budget Halloween pumpkin costume. Staggering out of the small fishbowl shaped holding cell, Joe walked up and leant on the man's desk with both his hands, facing him directly. The man smelt of cabbage and sunshine. A familiar smell.

"Um am I under arrest? What happened? Is Aileen alright?!" Questions tumbled out of Joe's mouth, starting as a soft mumble at first and ending in a raging shout.

Without flinching and remaining seated, only the man's lips moved as he spoke, "You've been through a lot today boy and I know you lost your parents only a few days ago"

The reminder of Joe's parent's recent death sent an emotional shiver down his spine, forcing Joe to look at his feet.

The man continued, "The garbage man found you passed out in a pool of blood and umm... faeces, among other things. We don't know where Aileen is, unless of course you can help us with that?"

Joe thought it through with all two of his remaining neurons firing at full speed. He knew it would be foolish of him to explain to the authorities that his Godmother was eaten by a demonic, autonomous dumpster. Without any evidence to back him up, Joe would be suspect number one. Suspect number two was about to reveal itself if Joe couldn't find a toilet fast enough.

"Ah no...sorry I thought you could tell me", Joe replied sheepishly. He didn't quite know where he has seen this deputy before, but there was something peculiar about him.

"Don't you worry boy. We'll have your clothes tested for any trace evidence and I'll keep a close eye out for Aileen. Do you have anywhere you can stay for the night?" The man sat as still as a mannequin engaged in an intense staring competition with a dead goldfish.

It was all too easy.

'Why am I being let go? Are they in on this?' Joe needed to keep his cool, he couldn't let the deputy know that he knew that the deputy knew about him knowing. No-one could know.

"Um yeah, Brandon Red's house. His parents are expecting me." Joe lied, "What time is it anyway?"

The man continued to stare directly ahead with only a small smirk breaking out of his otherwise frozen demeanour, "12pm boy, you'd best be going then."

Without saying another word, Joe grabbed his backpack and exited out the front door of the small station, not wanting to look back at the man in fear of looking guilty.

•

Joe and Brandon had a secret meetup location in case the other was ever late to a rendezvous. It was an abandoned warehouse on the opposite side of town from Joe's house, situated just outside the town's gated perimeter in the forbidden zone. Brandon was the only one who Joe could trust and the only one crazy enough to believe what happened to Aileen.

It wasn't a long walk, after all Doomsville's town is

only two square kilometres in size, with a stagnant population of just under five hundred. Joe kept his stroll casual as not to raise suspicion, carefully looking into the reflections of windows to see if he was being followed.

'Was Dad right to be paranoid all these years?', pondered Joe, as he walked down yet another empty street, 'He always spoke about strange changes in the town but no one else believed him!'

As hard as he tried not to, Joe couldn't help but stop at his old family home on Abomination Terrace. It's once colourful red and white paint was now hidden under a large grey dome which was covered in yellow biohazard tape. It had only been three days since the dreaded incident that cost him his parents, but for Joe it felt like a lifetime.

"What happened? Why did you leave me?!" Joe yelled out loud to the burnt shell of a once loved home, but no answer came, and Joe wasn't waiting around for one either.

After making a few dummy passes of the abandoned warehouse to ensure he wasn't being followed, Joe found the section of fence covered by tall grass that Brandon and he cut last year to get access into the forbidden zone. Like any good horror backstory, the warehouse was once used to store an unknown ultra-rare alien metal, that was quickly deemed too dangerous for human possession and removed from the site over a decade ago, nothing too ironical or plot driven I'm sure.

Joe approached the warehouse door with more caution than a Meerkat laced with amphetamines, listening for any footsteps or the subtle squeak of a plastic dumpster wheel. Joe bopped here, he slid there, he ducked under, he jumped over, and when he was finally finished with the 'Hop Scotch' drawn on the ground, he decided it was time to get serious.

"Oi!", bellowed a voice out of the bushes surrounding the rear of the warehouse.

Joe froze. This would be the second time today Joe needed to change his underwear.

Emerging from the bush was a gingered haired albino giant of a boy, with the biggest grin on his face. "So, let me guess, you went and saw Roxanne a little earlier than expected if you get my drift dude?", he exclaimed, seeming satisfied with himself as he chewed on a piece of long grass.

Joe unclenched his buttocks in relief. If there had been dirt somewhere in his pants, it had surely turned to diamonds under that amount of pressure.

"Ah Brandon, I am so glad to see you man", sighed

Joe, trying hard to hold the tears of relief back from Brandon's glaring eyes.

"Woah dude, what happened to you?", Brandon said as he moved close enough to see Joe was wearing prisoner issued clothes.

And so, they talked. Brandon cursed and Joe cried, until all the talking, cursing and tears were spent. By then two minutes had passed and they were prepared to put a plan in place. Inside the completely safe and in no way suspicious abandoned warehouse, they made their decision. The decision to fight!

"This is where we will lure that...that thing in", Brandon stuttered, choking on his words as he tried to get his head around the insane prospect.

Brandon got to work dragging in all the spare metal he could find from around the warehouse while Joe foraged for metal cables.

The question remained. What lures a dumpster out from hiding? What could be so compelling it would force a dumpster of artificial intelligence, to forego its programming and rush carelessly into a trap?

The answer was simple. Joe's socks.

While eagerly grabbing a second change of clothes earlier that day, Joe accidently picked a pair from the bottom of his Mt Everest of filthy clothes. Encased in the backpack and yet to be opened, was the smell of a hundred smells, the putrefaction of a thousand fish and the decomposition of a million used baby diapers. Joe was the lord of the pungent, the messiah of the malodorous and the emperor of the rancid. His sock selecting accident today could well turn the tide in the battle between good and evil.

Using Brandon's doomsday prepper bag left in the warehouse in case of emergencies, Brandon and Joe gloved up, masked up and barbeque tonged up.

"Dude, umm the rating on these masks is only like seven out of ten. Are you certain these can handle your socks?", squealed Brandon as his bravado suddenly shrivelled up like a prunes pruney testicles on a cold winter's day. And rightfully so.

Brandon was the unfortunate victim of Joe's caustic underwear disaster of 2016. On a sleepover that is now etched into Doomsville history, Brandon and Joe were camping out in Brandon's backyard when Joe casually flung his underwear out of his sleeping bag to get comfortable. For Joe's personal comfort, Brandon paid the ultimate price. The underwear hit the open flame and ignited instantaneously.

Some myths say Joe's underwear was worn for five

hundred consecutive days without a single wash. Others say the fabric held a pong so potent it was the equivalent to the fallout of an atomic bomb. All we know is that when the fine mist of the de-crustified underwear came raining down on an unsuspecting Brandon, he did what no-one should do. In a foolish attempt to protect himself, Brandon zipped his sleeping bag shut, locking himself in with the funky stench. His screams that night still haunt the neighbours' children to this day.

"Yeah man, don't stress hey. I can handle my own smells. You just make sure you have the trap ready", Joe said tentatively, hoping to boost Brandon's resolve. It was a blatant lie, but Joe couldn't have Brandon getting cold feet, he needed his 'A' game.

The trap was simple yet effective. A platform made of titanium strong enough to withstand the noxious odour was placed in the middle of the warehouse one meter off the ground. Tied to either side of the platform were two strong steel cables stretching outwards to either side of the warehouse. The cables were winched tight and ran up the walls to the ceiling, connected to a large net hanging above the platform that held over two tons of metal. It was your typical cartoon trap, what could go wrong?

Unzipping a small portion of the bag containing the

socks, unleashed a smell that hit Joe like a wall. Brandon standing ten meters back, was hit faster than the speed of sound, with a sonic blast rippling through the air.

"STAY WITH ME BRANDON!", Joe yelled, watching Brandon crouch down on the ground with his hands over his knees as he rocked back and forth sobbing uncontrollably. The Post Traumatic Stench Disorder had kicked in. Joe would have to go it alone.

Holding the BBQ tongs as hard as he could, Joe pulled a sock out gently, fighting wave upon wave of nausea. Each centimetre of the sock that was exposed amplified the stench factor tenfold. Eyes watering more than an enraged onion murdering its unfaithful onion wife, Joe looked down at his hands. The tongs quivering rapidly as the metal started to warp under the intense chemical reactions taking place.

Heart pounding loudly in his pigeon sized chest, Joe took one step closer to the platform before his knees buckled under the immense gravity of the pong.

'Just ten more steps, you can do it', Joe pleaded to himself. His gloves had disintegrated, exposing his arms which turned bright red, infected with some kind of super fungus that would require a power sander to remove.

"I BELIEVE IN YOU!", yelled Brandon, now rejuvenated at the other end of the warehouse, jumping in the air and pumping his fist.

Pushed on by Brandon's renewed energy, Joe plundered forward with the tongs now at one hundred degrees Celsius, evaporating Joe's dripping forehead sweat instantly. With only two steps to go Joe's knees gave in, knocking together like a bad dance move and dragging him to the ground.

Flat on his stomach with his arms stretched out in front of him, Joe was less than a meter from the platform when he saw the monster. In the shadows emerged two red eyes, followed by the squeak of plastic wheels.

'Gotchya now', thought Joe.

The Dumpster chose to stalk Joe from a distance at a conveniently slow pace. Its beady eyes flickered from red to green, a sure sign the pungent sock was impacting its decision processing system, drawing it closer to the densest waste product it had ever encountered.

The Dumpster was closing in on Joe, with its own rancid breath breaking through the barriers of the sock's stench field. Joe looked back at Brandon standing meters behind him, with his mouth wide open in awe and horror. Looking forward again, Joe saw that the Dumpster was less than a meter away now, arms ejecting outwards from its sides.

With all the effort he had left in his upper body, Joe pushed forward and flung the stiff sock at the platform like a double handed stinky shotput. The sock hit the plate, immediately warping the metal with its shape.

'Hold, hold...', Joe begged it like a begging beggar who begged his last beg.

The Dumpster wheeled onto the platform as if under a trance, picked up the sock with its clamps and devoured it like it was a delicious toe jam cherry. A long metallic prong ejected out from its lid and swiped left to right, licking its proverbial lips. But the platform remained intact.

"No! Break already you bastard! Hurry up and break!", Joe whimpered out loud, panic running through his mind as the Dumpsters eyes turned from green to red, preparing to fulfil its purpose-built duty of retrieving his brain.

Joe couldn't move. He felt as useless as a sentence describing how useless he really is, only to realize you have started reading that useless sentence and are continuing to waste further time reading it, knowing that the next part is just as useless as the first and so on. That's pretty useless.

Twice in one day Joe succumbed to defeat, a record even by the French Army standards. Joe looked back to where Brandon was before to tell him to run, save himself, or some other cliché yet admirable quote to tell his future children about. But not this time. Brandon wasn't there.

Darkness enveloped Joe again as the hot breath of the Dumpster drew closer, its cold metal clamp about to squeeze down on Joe's warm squishy scalp. Then from above came a deafening roar. Or more of a crackled teenage boy squeal. It was Brandon, and he was one angry ginger albino. A sight few live to see, or better yet tell the tale.

Brandon stood balanced on the metal beam near the winched cable and in a display of raw intimidation, ripped his shirt off straight down the middle, exposing white skin so bright it ignited the warehouse in a supernova of light. Using his shirt as a flying fox handle, Brandon wrapped it around the nearest metal cable and jumped down from the beam with surprising speed and agility. Joe knew he could count on Brandon for his physical prowess.

Brandon at only fifteen years of age, standing at six-foot five inches tall, weighing in at a solid one hundred kilograms, had stepped in to save Joe's smelly behind on many occasions. Normally there would be ample time to have one of those origin story flashbacks, a warm and fuzzy memory of when Joe and Brandon first met. But not today, for Brandon had miss timed his swing.

Ever watched a great white shark jump out of the water to spectacularly take out an unsuspecting seal, then dive back into the sea with beautiful grace? Change shark to 'dumpster', jump with 'extend its metallic prong', water to 'from its lid', unsuspecting seal with 'Brandon', dive back to 'retract its metallic prong', and beautiful grace with 'horrific savagery'. No? Not descriptive enough for you?

Fine. I understand. As you the reader and loyal customer come first, at least let me get some fresh air before delving into this depraved curiosity you have with explicit details. Use this time to reflect on yourself. For shame.

Ok, let's set the mood for you. Cue the sad slow violins with a solitary piano piece and a choir full of angelic voices humming softly in the background. Change the filter to black and white. Reduce the speed to slow motion. Sit back and relax, you heathen.

Brandon stretched both his legs out in front during his mid-swing to kick the Dumpster's lid, hoping to put more pressure on the plate to break the cables and release the net. Like a cobra rearing its ugly head, the Dumpsters metallic prong shot out from inside its lid at a lightning pace. It was two meters long and separated into segments, each of which ended with a jagged sharp tip resembling a foot-long stingray barb.

The barb impaled the top of Brandon's left leg with violent force, plunging through his flesh like an overweight kid performing a belly flop in a paddling pool. Pushing out the other side of his leg, pieces of Brandon's muscle and cartilage sprayed out in the air like confetti, but not the kind you would want at your wedding. Brandon screamed out in agony as the barb re-adjusted itself mid-flight and skewered itself into his other leg, creating a Brandon kebab.

Dangling upside down like a cheap piñata, Brandon passed out from the shock before being ceremoniously lowered down into the Dumpsters open lid, its red eyes fixated on Brandon's now expressionless face. Revitalized from his panic, Joe jumped to his feet and ran to the nearest winched cable, picked up a hatchet and began hacking away at the metal cable as furiously as he could.

His efforts were all in vain. Joe looked over to the Dumpster only to see Brandon's feet dangling out of the top of the lid, jerking from left to right as the Dumpster made an unusual noise that sounded like a mixture between a washing machine cycle and a blender. Joe kept hacking away with tears running down his face, but this time tears of anger.

'You won't die for nothing Brandon', Joe assured himself, his arms numb from the metal on metal reverberations after striking the cable over and over again.

Just as the cable was on its last steel thread, Joe saw the metallic prong extending back outwards in his peripherals, holding something very red. The Dumpster had somehow reconfigured its compactification process to act like a fine shredder, carefully skinning Brandon and leaving only his bare muscles and tendons. It held Brandon's lifeless body upwards like a meaty trophy.

The horror. The unimaginable horror. The unimaginable, unfathomable horror. But Joe could fathom it. And Joe didn't need to imagine it either. Brandon's eyes stared at Joe, but without his eyelids he couldn't tell if he was dead or alive. Without waiting to find out, Joe struck the last remaining thread as hard as his under developed arms could.

The weight of two tons of scrap metal came crashing down on the Dumpster harder than a Flat Earthers theory of the Solar System. Metal, blood, organs and oil created a splatter effect that spray painted the warehouse a new colour. The colour of death. Joe could see the crumpled mass of what was left of the Dumpster, intertwined with the dismembered corpse of his once best friend.

With no tears left to shed, Joe felt a wave of accomplishment wash over him. Slowly walking out of the warehouse and back through the fence without a single look back, Joe breathed a sigh of relief.

'It's over', Joe reassured his petrified thoughts.

And like every naive main character in a mainstream horror story before him, he thought he was right.

●

Sliding like a sneaky salamander after a salacious encounter, the sinister Servant of Sins slunk through the shadows of the silent warehouse. Stroking his supernatural invention, the Son of Satan spoke spell like scripture to sustain the savage Dumpsters seemingly broken spirit.

"Soon", spoke the Saint of Spitefulness, stretching his speech to summon the souls of vanquished foes.

"Soooooooon"

Chapter Three
It Has To End...or does it?

It's not too late to end this story here. Put this book down now, retain your sanity and return to your humble, yet predictably dull lives. Finish on a high note and forget that the remaining pages contain only woe and misery. Surely the last two chapters have wasted only a meagre half hour or so of your pathetically boring existence? That's a good exchange for escapism don't you think? You don't need to invest any more time in this sadistic venture, wouldn't you agree?

No?

Excellent. If I had hands, I would be rubbing them together in the most conniving and mischievous way, like a chimpanzee at the zoo who secretly threw its faeces into your unsuspecting chocolate soft serve ice-cream and is eagerly awaiting your first bite. Diabolical, but I digress.

Joe walked through a haze of uncertainty, not knowing whether he should feel relief, or grieve for the loss of his best friend. It was a slow walk back to his street with every step longer than the last. Deep thoughts penetrated his surroundings and obscured the reality he found himself in.

'How do I move on from all this? What was this all about? Why was I targeted?', Joe interrogated his exhausted brain, waterboarding his sub-conscious with forced questions.

It wasn't until he reached his blood-stained house that Joe remembered his final event planned for the day.

"Roxanne!", Joe exclaimed out loud, jumping in the air like an over excited hamster receiving a new exercise wheel. Embarrassed with his display, Joe looked around. An empty street again. Not a soul.

Choosing to ignore this blatantly obvious plot point, Joe turned around one hundred and eighty degrees, pivoting harder than a one-legged ice skater in a Congo line and sprinted down the street towards the cinema.

'I need this', Joe urged to himself, 'After the day I've had, I'm going to tell Roxanne how I really feel about her'.

The tale of Joe and Roxanne could be played out like Romeo and Juliet in Joe's mind. In reality, Joe was as romantically capable as a three-day old chicken nugget laying on your kitchen floor, which requires sheer desperation to even contemplate eating it.

And desperate was Joe's middle name.

Joe had been locked into the friend zone with Roxanne longer than most people get jail time for murder. But not today, not if Joe could help it. Today, he was going to man up and beat his chest to the rhythm of love.

Feet pounding on the gravel road, heart thumping out of his chest and arms flailing like an inflatable waving tube man at a second-hand car dealership, Joe was nearing the cinema. As he turned the corner, the large standalone building appeared before him. An old red brick relic from the 1960's, with a broken-down neon sign that once said, "DOOM NIGHT-GOERS", but today the O, M, IGH and ERS letters were all blacked out. But whatever you do, don't read into that.

This small run down, single screen complex was the only cinema Doomsville ever had. The local government passed a ban in 1985 on all science fiction movies, following a controversial time travel movie release, where the plot relied on travelling to the past to correct the future. As if anyone would come up with a plotline as mundane as that...am I right?

The citizens were told the reason behind this ban

was so that they could live their peaceful lives without any unrealistic expectations of fantasy. And like the collective slave mind they were, they believed it.

Joe dug his heels into the grassed area just in front of the cinema's glass doors, braking harder than an unsuspecting chicken, who walked into the kitchen only to find his mother slowly rotating over a fire.

There in the front concession booth, awaiting guests with tickets and beverages, was a man who looked very much like the deputy from the police station. This time, he had a thick fake moustache, mirrored aviator glasses and what appeared to be a wig with a rear mullet, but Joe was certain it was him. The same familiar smell of cabbage and sunshine wafted in the air as he drew closer. And that scar...that scar he just couldn't place. The strange man didn't move a muscle, staring at Joe more intently than an illiterate person attempting to read the dictionary cover to cover.

Not wanting to raise suspicions with the strange man, Joe kept his head down low, approached the booth and asked in a whisper, "One ticket please".

The strange man rolled up his red and white chequered sleeves exposing thick black hair on his wiry arms and pulled a small piece of yellow paper from his top left breast pocket. "I believe this is for you boy, a cute little thing name Roxanne left it here only 15 minutes ago."

Joe snatched the paper and turned his back on the booth to read the note in private.

JOE. I'VE HAD A CHANGE OF HEART, LET'S MEET AT RUBBISH DUMP RIDGE AND WATCH THE SUNSET. ROXY

Joe was so ecstatic with this change of plan that the fact Roxanne never calls herself Roxy didn't cross his mind. But as any teenage boy in Doomsville knew, the most romantic place of all was 'Make-out dump ridge', the only place in the whole town that allowed you to get a glimpse of the outside world beyond the gated perimeter. After the first few deep inhales of the rotting rubbish pushed you past your gag reflex, couples would lock lips and talk about what they would do if they could get out of this town, if only for a day.

Joe turned back around to thank this mysterious man, but the booth was empty. With a shrug of his shoulders and clouded with pubescent hormones imagining his first kiss with Roxanne, Joe skipped back the way he came. The Sun was slowly setting in the East, illuminating the sky with red tipped clouds that oozed across the horizon like Brandon's mangled corpse across the warehouse floor…

The thought stopped Joe in his tracks if only for a moment, as he shook his head violently, slapping his forehead with both hands in an effort to dissolve the memories from his mind.

'East?' Joe cleared his fragile but sharp cognitive functions for a moment. The Sun was setting in the East, contrary to Doomsville's geographical location that you will never find out about. Joe closed his eyes, squeezing them harder than a lemon squeezer squeezing the squeeziest lemon it could squeeze. Opening his eyes like a new born baby for the first time, Joe saw that the Sun was in fact setting in the West now.

Don't you even think about that glitch being important to the books ending, you spoiler junkie!

'It's been a big day, don't lose your grip Joe', he begged himself, as he broke into a slow jog through the empty Doom Street and towards the cul-de-sac that held the entry to the towns Rubbish Dump.

The Rubbish Dump was Doomsvilles greatest achievement. It had a perfectly circular layout, much like the town plan and housed several state-of-the-art recycling stations, each separated at five different points. This pentagram of ingenuity powered the entire town. While the Rubbish Dump was open to the public, no one was allowed to step foot inside the recycling stations which ran autonomously since their anonymous invention.

No one knew who invented them or how they were powered themselves, only that they were off limits. Maybe it's aliens? No, it's never aliens…

Walking past the entry bollards, Joe saw the back of a man dressed in green overalls tending to a nearby rubbish truck engine bay. Joe caught a glimpse of the man looking at him in the corner of his eye.

'Impossible!' Joe screamed in his head, spinning around to look at the same man who was at the cinema, the very same man who was also at the police station. This time he was attempting to camouflage himself with thick reading glasses and a terrible excuse of a bald cap. However, he couldn't hide that long scar across his face.

"WHY ARE YOU FOLLOWING ME?!", Joe bellowed with a fury that surprised even himself. None of this day made sense to him and he had lost all patience with pretending not to notice this strange man. He stood there shocked, his mouth open as if ready to spill the truth when Joe heard an ear-piercing scream.

"Roxanne?" Joe spun around, feeling like a turn table after an alcohol fuelled turn table orgy, as he desperately scouted the dump site to determine the source of the fleeting sound.

Another scream ran out across the dump, this time with a curdle at the end, like the sound the kitchen sink makes as the last dregs of food force the water to bubble upwards.

A large building in the centre of the recycle stations had its front steel door ajar, emitting the painful scream outwards directly into Joe's inner ear, radiating down to his extremities in a cold tingle of dread. Joe whipped his head on a swivel to where the strange man was last standing, only to see he had disappeared yet again.

'It has to be him, he must be *The Master* the Dumpster spoke of', thought Joe.

Slowly and carefully approaching the front door to the central building, Joe scanned his surroundings as the dwindling light faded, creating ominous shapes from the shadows cast off the towering piles of rubbish.

Joe didn't want to rush in knowing this was now a trap, he wanted the only advantage he had left to be of some use. The advantage was he knew Roxanne would already be dead and there would be nothing he could do to stop that now. *The Master* would be waiting.

Near the entry to the door rested a large commercial sized wrench so heavy Joe had to use both hands to wield it. Swinging it over his right shoulder and stepping through the door, Joe allowed his eyes to adjust to the red light that filled the interior. Whatever pitiful muscles Joe had on his body were now engorged with blood, tensed and ready to strike. He wouldn't go down without a fight, not this time.

Half a dozen red lanterns swung from the circular building's ceiling in unison, highlighting several bronze cylinders each pulsating with green static. At the centre of the room was a black metallic structure no bigger than a double garage shed. The structure had a long conveyor belt leading into its entrance and a steel roller door that opened and closed intermittently. When the door opened, Joe could see an immense blue fire erupting inside, the heat was so hot it was burning his skin from fifty meters away.

As Joe cautiously stepped closer, he was expecting the unexpected, preparing for the unpreparable and completely losing all bladder control. Each footstep made a soft squelching noise similar to a suspiciously wet fart in the rain. Joe didn't want to look down as he felt the moistness of the ground soaking into his socks and up his pant legs. Not wanting to wade through this unknown substance any further, Joe called out his foe.

"I'm here. You wanted me. Well now you have me. Show yourself!"

Silence.

Squelch.

Squelch.

Silence.

"Welcome Joe. Ha haaaaa...", came an over the top, over acted, deep booming laugh echoing across the buildings circular walls.

"Now would you be so kind as to put down that wrench and let me take what is rightfully mine. Your BRAIN!" screeched *The Master*, remaining in the shadows as he moved from one cylinder to the next, throwing Joe's sensory system into chaos.

Hands clenched around the wrench in rage, sweat beading down his face and teeth gritted together, Joe snarled with all the hate he had in his once pure heart, "You're going to have to take it from my cold dead body".

"Tssk Tssk my dear child, but there is no other way I can! Didn't you ever take Human Biology lessons? While I'm endeared by your courage, there is no use fighting your fate any longer. Let me introduce you to my servant of evil, you have both been acquainted twice today already. This will be the last time you meet", said *The Master* as eloquently as a sleazy door salesman, attempting to sell you the latest and greatest vacuum cleaner for just five easy payments. I said he was evil, I never said he was good at it.

As the roller shutter opened once more the blue light shone out, highlighting a large metal object in front, with a dark cloaked figure standing beside it, stroking its dome shaped lid.

"How? I destroyed that...that DEMON!", Joe stammered, tightening his grip on the wrench, planting his legs as firmly as he could in the jelly like ground under his feet.

"Bahaha you cannot destroy that which isn't alive. I gave this precious object a purpose through powers that you can never comprehend. And speaking of which, I do hope you enjoy the 'Roxanne Fertilizer' my loyal subject scattered generously around this building. His woodchipper function came in handy when Roxanne refused to assist us in luring you here. Now she too has a...GRATER...purpose ha ha haaaaa!", cackled *The Master* to his own cheap humour.

Looking ever so slowly down at his feet, Joe saw one

of Roxanne's once beautiful blue eyes staring back, stuck in a large Roxanne puree that had been liberally spread around the entire floor.

Joe stared back at *The Master*, desperate to see what was under that dark hooded robe and stepped closer to the Dumpster without fear this time, only anger. "Why me? Just tell me that much, you monstrous piece of shit!"

"Uhhh, I'm bored of this. Kill him my Dumpster of Doom and bring me his brain unharmed", quipped *The Master*, clearly using the title of this Part in the book to emphasize his dramatic effect.

The Dumpster began its slow wheel of death around one side of the conveyor belt, as Joe began his own on the other side, destined to meet at the centre.

"I know who you are", Joe stated out loud keeping his voice steady and firm. For once he was in control.

"I know it was you at the Police Station, the Cinema and then here near the Rubbish truck. I know your face. You don't scare me", Joe paced through the swampy meat of Roxanne's remains and neared the mouth of the conveyor belt. He watched the Dumpster from across the other side of the room wheeling its way through Roxanne's sludge with ease, as fresh blood dribbled down its lid staining its newly reconstructed sides.

"What? You fool, that wasn't me. Been having many glitches' today? Seeing things that aren't there? I bet you have you poor, poor soul. Never mind, it'll all be over soon", pouted the arrogant *Master*, now leaning against the side of the metallic furnace with his arms folded in a display of premature victory.

Joe stopped meters away from the mouth of the belt as the Dumpster made its slow turn around the corner.

'This doesn't make sense. Everything pointed to that man. I need to find out. I must find out!', Joe demanded of himself.

This would have to be a slug fest. In order to beat the Dumpster, Joe knew he would have to pulverize it piece by piece, all the while avoiding its deadly arms and its barbed prong.

"For Aileen. For Brandon. And for ROXANNE!", belted Joe, wrench raised in the air like a Germanic Barbarian in Roman times.

"JOE!!" Yelled an unknown voice from the building's entry door.

With the Dumpster nearing its next turn, Joe angled his head ever so slightly to look in the direction of the voice, not sure if this was another trick set by

The Master.

It was the man. The strange man. The strange and now unmasked, unbearded, unwigged, non-aviator wearing man standing by the door, his hand hovering over a large and glaringly obvious green button attached to the wall.

"Find me again…this morning. Find me this morning!", said the strange man with a hint of pride in his voice.

Joe squinted like a suspicious elderly lady spying on the nudist neighbours through the curtains, trying hard to get a clearer image of the man through the sweat stinging his eyes.

"What does that even mean?", Joe questioned out loud.

"Don't you even think about it you son of a motherless ham!" exclaimed *The Master*, now pacing towards the doors with his dark cloak flowing behind him like wisps of smoke. His face was still covered under the hood with a strangely bulbous shaped head stretching the fabric to its limits.

The strange man pushed the green button and ran out of view. The conveyor belt started instantaneously. Large industrial strength suction plugs placed at every few meters rotated along the belt, each plug was used to carry heavy pieces of scrap metal into the structures furnace.

The Dumpster stopped at the mouth the belt, extended its arms and attempted in vain to remove a plug now attached to its underside, slowly dragging it onto the platform. It pulled. It pushed. It shoved. It heaved. It failed.

Joe dropped the heavy wrench to his side, took a large step back as the Dumpster slid alongside him, extending its probe in a last ditched effort to grab hold of him, its barbs scratching his cheek as he turned his head away from the glancing blow.

The Master ran back to the opposite side of the structure, black gloves on top of his hooded head in defeat, watching his inventions slow demise as it was dragged into the open mouth of the furnace.

"I…AM…SORRY…MASTERRRRRR", bellowed its automated voice, as the blue fire consumed it and the roller shutter closed.

"You have done NOTHING to stop me except waste my time!", screeched *The Master*, slowly stepping backwards into the cover of darkness surrounding the cylinders.

Joe walked around the conveyor belt, stalking *The Master* step for step.

"Tell me who you are? Why me?", Joe expelled through gritted teeth, knowing he now had the upper hand.

"Ha ha! This isn't the first time we have done this dance, nor will it be our last. In time, I will perfect the extraction of your brain, but at least for now, you won't remember a thing! You have only delayed the inevitable, postponed the unstoppable and put a layby on your own death. See you soon bwahahaha", sung *The Master* as he edged into the shadows, allowing them to consume him entirely.

Joe sprinted into the darkness after *The Master*, swinging wildly at the blackness, cursing to the heavens and hoping he had made contact. After several laps of the building, Joe fell to his knees, breathing heavier than a stalker leaving a voice mail message to his victim.

"I'LL NEVER FORGET!" Joe screamed desperately through muffled sobs of despair, kneeling with arms out wide pleading like the protagonist should at this stage in the story.

"NEVERRRRR!" he screamed again, this time for added effect.

•

Staggering into his house later that night, Joe was

mentally broken and physically ruined. As he dragged his non-responsive legs up the spiral staircase, Joe kept thinking of the strange man who saved him.

'But what does it mean, find me again this morning? That's impossible. Maybe he meant tomorrow morning?', questioned Joe in his mind.

Joe knew he would have to find the strange man again. He would have the answers he sought. 'Tomorrow', Joe told himself, as he fell backwards onto his bed, sprawled out like a drunken cat trying to clean its genitals. 'I'll find the man tomorrow and we'll fight *The Master* together'

With fond memories of Aileen, Brandon and Roxanne slipping in and out of his sub-conscious mind, Joe let the sweet taste of sleep overcome him and sooth his troubled thoughts.

•

Advantageously assessing his adversary, this Architect of Annihilation arranged an even deadlier assassin to await his altered assault plan. Already alive with the assistance of archaic powers, and alliteration...the Arbiter of Abominations allied himself accordingly, and with anonymity as his aggressor, he applied his Anti-Christ style anger around his aptitude for being the most absolute

Arch nemeses around.

Feverishly fixated on finalizing his next fiendish and frightful Frankenstein like foe, this Frontrunner of Fear is ready yet again to fight. Fortune favours this Figurehead of Fatalities, as he formulates another freakish and fun-filled foil proof plan full of foreboding, forthwith.

•

Waking from his dreamless sleep, Joe Brown stretched his extremities until he felt his bones pop and clambered out of his dilapidated single bed. Looking across his jail sized room, Joe caught a glimpse of the time from his retro Casio watch, with built in calculator might I add.

7:55am, Saturday.

He waited for a moment for the feeling of déjà vu to dissipate, hanging over him like a cheap strawberry scented air freshener that a homeless man has wiped with his arse, and placed on your car's review mirror.

"Breakfast is ready Joe", a voice echoed from downstairs.

'Ah, smells like bacon.' Joe loved bacon...

PART II
THE TOASTER OF TERROR

Chapter Four

It Has Begun…Again?

Racing down the spiral staircase, Joe couldn't shake his feeling of trepidation. Shortly after being 'Baconned' again, Joe sat down at the rickety two-seater dining room table with Aileen's old cane for a chair leg on one end, and her ex-husbands prosthetic leg holding up the other.

Chewing on the rubbery piece of month-old bacon used to lure him downstairs, Joe couldn't help but stare in awe at Aileen as she hovered over her makeshift stove, which was just a large forty-four-gallon drum with a steel grate on top, squeezed into the area the oven used to be before Aileen's accident involving chopsticks and a llama. I'll get to that story eventually.

'Why does it feel like I'm still sleeping?', Joe questioned himself, frowning as he scraped the cockroach eggs off his tongue which had jettisoned themselves off the bacon.

"Beef and squid eye porridge, your favourite", Aileen stated proudly as she waddled over from the small dank kitchen like a zombie emperor penguin.

With a large pot full of the rancid mix under her goblin like arm, she slopped Joe's portion into his empty bowl with the sound of a cow patty falling from a ten-story building. Joe winced and gave Aileen his best impression of a grateful smile, resembling more of a constipated goldfish staring down a starving feline. If Aileen caught just a glimpse of Joe's distaste for the porridge, then he would have to face down her ultimate culinary specialty instead. Ratatouille. Where the meat is actual rat, the sauce is Aileen's used bathtub water, and vegetables that comprised of her toenails mixed with a garnish of grated bunions. Yes, yummy yummy porridge it is for Joe.

"I have something even more special for you today Joey my boy!", Aileen said through her brown gummy smile.

'Oh no! Not another surprise', Joe pleaded in his head.

Ever since Aileen attempted to surprise him for his thirteenth birthday with underwear she stole from a homeless man, only later to find out that it contained ten generations of lice living in the soiled crutch, Joe went out of his way to politely, yet cautiously let Aileen know her 'surprises' were not needed.

"Really it's ok Aileen! This porridge is delicious, mmm mmm...I couldn't possibly need anything else!", Joe begged, intentionally shoving three spoonsful of the putrid goop in his mouth, leaving beef entrails and squid eye tendons dribbling down his face.

Turning her haggard, lump ridden back to Joe, Aileen cackled out loud. "Oh, don't be silly my dear boy, this is something I haven't had the luxury of eating in years. Trust me, you'll be...dying...to have some."

Joe was puzzled. More puzzled then a puzzle *Master*, whose last puzzle puzzled him into a permanent puzzling state of puzzlement. That's very puzzling.

'Something isn't right', Joe queried to himself as he looked around the dining room no bigger than a jail cell, expecting someone or something to jump out at him.

Aileen was holding a metallic box in her hand as she moved around the kitchen with all the grace of a beached walrus rolling in the sand.

As if in tune with his sixth sense, Joe jumped to his feet with adrenaline surging through his veins preparing him to fight. Joe looked down at his hands clenched into baby sized fists, shocked by his subconscious reaction. He had always been a quiet and timid child, never prone to violence.

Joe interrogated his mind like a barbaric medieval torturer, 'Why do I feel this way? What's wrong with me?'

Aileen turned around, the grey metal object tucked under her arm and a smile of satisfaction on her face that quickly turned sour.

"What are you doing Joey! Sit back down, I told you I have a surprise. Some lovely stranger sent us a gift this morning. It said on the box we won it in a raffle!", Aileen snapped, causing Joe's knees to buckle in submission and fall back onto his cardboard box seat.

The metallic box came crashing down onto the wobbly table top as Aileen walked away with a cord attached to its rear, looking for a power socket amongst the ten overflowing litter trays stacked against the wall.

"Uh, a toaster?" Joe asked, more puzzled now than a ridiculous sentence describing how puzzled he felt.

"Yes!", Aileen gleamed, as proud as a deviant who used a display-only toilet at the local hardware store to release their bowels, while suspiciously looking around before closing the lid and slowly sneaking away.

"And look! It's one of those fancy dual toasters like they made when I was a little girl", Aileen remarked smugly, looking up and to the left in a nostalgic haze as if she was looking back into time itself.

"HA! Little girl!", scoffed Joe, choking on his words as he realized he said it out loud.

CRACK!

He didn't stand a chance. Searing pain engulfed Joe's senses as he placed both hands on his pimpled face. Aileen's tea towel shaved Joe's left eyebrow clean off at a speed faster than a frog's tongue grabbing its prey, leaving only red raw skin in its place.

"Let that be a warning! Next comment like that and I'll turn YOU into a little girl!", Aileen bellowed, her thick Irish accent intensifying with her anger.

Like a shy kid on his first day at school who plunged his own head in the toilet to save the bullies time, Joe kept his head low as he inspected the toaster, trying his best not to make eye contact with Aileen. Joe rotated the toaster around in his sweaty damp hands and thought to himself, 'No brand name or manufacturer label? That's a bit weird'.

Shrugging his shoulders as the memories of his last toast breakfast drew him away, Joe placed the toaster back on the table while Aileen took a nose dive into the kitchens overflowing garbage bin, both of her deformed legs dangling off the ground.

"Arghhhh!", Aileen screeched, her scream muffled by the mountains of used ear buds which contained so much ear gunk they could start their own live wax museum.

Joe jumped to his feet ready for action and once again perplexed by his body's response.

'Jesus, maybe I'm playing too many video games', Joe thought to himself, relaxing all of his known sphincter muscles and sitting back down as Aileen pulled herself free from the bins deadly grasp, holding two pieces of bread above her head with a look of victory and faeces on her face. Lots and lots of cat faeces.

Flicking the last of Mr. Fluffington's cat excrement off her witch shaped bobble nose, Aileen began to scrape off the one-inch thick layer of green slimy mould from the bread slices.

"Good as new", she remarked, hobbling to the table and placing them into their own slice receivers in the toaster.

"Come to think of it, I never did enter a raffle", Aileen pondered out loud, pressing down the bread depressor and setting the toast level to a disturbing 9 out of 10, a heat hot enough to split atoms.

The small gun metal grey toaster no bigger than a tissue box, started to shudder violently. It had two triangular shaped lights glowing red on either side of the circular heat knob, with a thin black crumb catcher tray under that. One could say it resembled a rudimentary face. One could say that the face had the look of evil. One could also say it looks just like an ordinary toaster and you are reading too much into it. That person obviously never read the title of this Part!

With a jaw dropped lower than a dwarf doing the limbo and mouth open wide like a python at a hot dog eating contest, Joe let the magnificent smell of the toast consume him. Looking like a cartoon mummy with his arms out in front ready to receive the deliciousness that awaited, Joe made the fatal mistake of closing his eyes.

"Noooooooooo!", Aileen screamed like a banshee.

Joe felt her raptor hands push his body clean off the cardboard box seat, sending him halfway across the room with more force than a female Russian powerlifter with a questionable Adam's apple.

Joe lifted himself back to his feet, feeling more tender than a piece of steak caught in a physically abusive relationship. Turning around, Joe saw the dining table destroyed and Aileen lying in the middle of the rubble. There was a perfect semi-circle of blood splatter on either side of her body, trailing up the walls and onto the ceiling.

Staggering over, Joe could see her brown potato sack dress now had a thick red line of blood across her stomach. The skin was peeled back on either side with her small intestines spooling out meter by meter onto the floor.

"NO! What happened? Tell me what to do?!", Joe pleaded, confused about how this happened and desperately looking around the room for anything that could explain her injuries.

"Joe…", coughed Aileen, blood spraying upwards in a fine mist as she reached out her arm and grabbed his crumpled T-shirt, pulling him down onto one knee beside her.

"The toaster…it tried to kill you…with its toast…you need to run!", Aileen begged as more and more of her intestines flowed out like a can of human spaghetti, speeding away from her body on the slippery concrete floor.

"Huh? The Toaster? That's impossible...", Joe cut himself short as a small grey object peeked over the kitchen counter onto the broken table. The Toaster began to shudder violently again, its red eyes fixated on him.

From the ground, Aileen grabbed Joe by the ears and pulled him down towards her chest as a piece of toast projectile came flying out of the bread receiver, spinning like a ninja star with its four edges burnt down to deadly sharp spikes.

Joe's head slipped off Aileen's bloodied dress and plunged neck deep into her open stomach cavity. From inside Aileen's carcass he could hear a slashing noise and felt her hands release her grip on Joe. With both hands pressing on her abdomen, Joe pulled his head back out of her open wound and wiped her stomach lining from his eyes.

The piece of toast had narrowly missed Joe and ripped through Aileen's jugular, causing blood to pump out of her body faster than a rotating sprinkler. Joe placed his hands on her wounds as Aileen's eyes rolled to the back of her head.

"Don't you dare die on me Aileen! You're all I have", Joe wept as his tears mixed with the coagulated blood on his cheeks, creating a horrifying face mask without the healing benefits of cucumber.

"Come closer", Aileen gurgled to Joe, in a typical last words kind of response you would expect from a dying person.

Joe lent in closer, careful not to remove his hands from the wound on her neck.

"Joe... your parents... they didn't die...in a-"

"-cliché and unimportant way...", Joe interrupted, caught in a trance-like state with the words spilling out of his mouth.

Aileen smiled up at Joe, or at least he thought it was a smile. It could have been searing agony at the severe pain she was enduring with the half a dozen or so cats who had begun tearing away at her now external organs, dragging them off into different corners of the house to feed.

"I'm glad...you know", Aileen's voice trailed away, leaving behind one last gasp while forcefully flinging her head back and sticking her tongue out to the side, reminiscent of a bad actor attempting a death scene.

"But I don't know why I said that! Stay with me Aileen", appealed Joe to her lifeless shell.

"NO BREAD. I NEED MORE BREAD", came a robotic yet demonic voice.

Joe leapt to his feet and raced up to the kitchen,

looking over the counter and onto the floor. He could see the Toaster bouncing around, using a small arm extended from its bread depressor switch to sift through piles of rubbish. The Toaster wasn't connected to any power source, with its cord trailing behind it.

"You little shit!", yelled Joe, looking around for a weapon to arm himself with.

The Toaster stopped in its tracks, slowly turned its body around until its red eyes locked onto Joe's, tilting its head to the side like a curious reptile.

"I NEED MORE BREAD...SO I CAN GET YOUR BRAIN!", it shrieked, leaning on its depressor switch and flinging itself high in the air, while performing a sideways summersault through the kitchen window, shattering the glass as it spun through.

Stunned and in shock, Joe stood up with his arms locked by his side, staring blankly out the broken window.

'Bread for my brain? What the hell?', but before Joe could collect his thoughts, the front door bell rang.

Stalking the front door and pushing his back against the wall, Joe slid sideways like a mentally challenged assassin, looking for any clue of who it might be by peeking out the lounge room window. Parked out the front of the house was a red and black 'Ambo-Doom' Ambulance.

"Ah nah, we're all fine here thanks", lied Joe, "We didn't call you guys, maybe it's the house next door."

Joe knew that without the murderous Toaster he looked completely guilty. Turning back to look at Aileen's corpse which was now under attack by all fifteen cats, diving in and out of her open wound cavity and comparing meat chunks with each other, as they marked their territory on significant body parts with urine and faeces.

"I know you didn't call boy", said a familiar male voice from the other side of the rotting wooden door. "But no-one else will believe you about the Toaster! I know what happened. Let me in, I can help."

Hesitating more than a sloth playing a rigged game of Russian Roulette, Joe edged backwards and forwards until he reached the door handle, grabbing it by his left hand and keeping his other hand gripped firmly around the crowbar which leant against the wall.

Wrenching the door back as hard as he could, Joe pushed himself behind it so the man couldn't see him. He watched two black military boots slowly walk into the room. Once the boots passed the door, Joe slammed it with all his might, lifting the crowbar up above his head as menacingly as he could.

The man spoke softly without even looking back at Joe, "Now I know you didn't do this boy, but I have to get you out of here. I'm not your enemy". And with both arms up in submission the strange man turned around, flicking his magnificent mullet-

"YOU!", Joe yelled in supranger, rudely interrupting the narrator's description.

What's surpranger you ask? Surprise and anger, my unlearned friend. Please try to keep up!

"Sorry boy, but I need to do this", said the strange man with a hint of sincerity in his deep gruff voice.

Before Joe could reply, the strange man drove a syringe into his neck with the speed of a manic mongoose, plunging Joe's world into darkness.

•

Chapter Five

It's Just a Jump to the Left...

Ears ringing as if caught between two large percussion instruments in an orchestra, Joe awoke from his drug induced paralysis, feeling like a large plush teddy bear on the inside but with skin stickier then melted toffee apples on the outside.

Blinking his eyes faster than a fugitive hummingbird on the run for murder, Joe let the bright light eat away at his blurred vision, bringing the interior of an old run-down Ambulance into focus. Joe tried to lift himself the medical stretcher, but both his arms and legs were tied down to the gurney with a generous amount of first aid tape.

Joe could only just see out the front windscreen of the Ambulance. Lifting his egg-shaped head as high as he could, he could see they were parked near the fence line opposite the abandoned warehouse.

The strange man's voice came from behind Joe's head and whispered, "I'm sorry I had to do this to you boy, it was the only way and time is running out". The sound of two doors opening and shutting followed, causing Joes jelly like body to shudder uncontrollably.

"What the hell do you want with me? My brain? You won't be the first to ask for it today!", Joe lisped like a drunken anteater as he tried to fight the sedatives, spraying his surroundings in a copious amount of spit.

"Oh god no, not at all", gasped the strange man, his reflective aviators coming into Joe's focus as he felt tugging at his extremities.

Joe managed to angle his head to the right, he could see the tape was now removed from his arms and legs. The strange man now sat across from him, less than a meter away in the cramped rusted interior.

"I only tied you up to prevent you from falling off the stretcher, nothing more", the strange man gently insisted, putting both hands up with palms facing Joe.

Taking his time like a wary Chameleon unsure of its footings, Joe slowly sat up and pushed his back against the opposite side of the cabin, careful not to glance too often at the exits and give his plan of escape away. He waited instead for the blood to pump back into his semi-alert muscles.

Silence ensued for several painful minutes as Joe stared into the expressionless face of the strange man in front of him. Joe was angry, confused and much worse than that, he was constipated. I'm not talking of your run of the mill every day constipation. Oh no, that's a walk in the proverbial colon park compared to what Joe had waiting in his lower intestine.

The diabolical dung Joe was holding onto was the second densest material known to Earth. Thanks to a mixture of Aileen's last few unspeakable meals and Joe's quite literal gut-wrenching escapades of late, his digestive tract twisted into a poopified pretzel of pain. The composition of this criminal caca, whilst nearly enough to distract a novice reader for almost a paragraph, was not enough to prevent Joe from pursuing the identity and intentions of this strange man.

"You sent that Toaster after me, didn't you? Why me?", Joe's voice wavered as he struggled to remain in control, not wanting the strange man to know how terrified he really was. If his voice didn't give it away, the following nervous fart almost certainly did.

Placing a hand on his cheek and stroking his thick red scar, the strange man appeared empathetic, if only for a moment. It was most likely the noxious odour that snapped him out of it.

"Jesus Christ penguin balls!", the strange man yelled, waving his hairy arms in the air, attacking Joe's near solid fart with karate chops.

"Nothing I can say will make any of this easier for you boy", coughed the strange man, composing himself. "I think its best I show you and then you'll know who's side I'm on."

And with that the strange man stood up, his wide barrel chest taking up all the remaining room between them. Pushing the rear Ambulance doors open and jumping outside, the strange man disappeared from view.

With a full range of mobility back under his control, including his recently embattled rectum, Joe leapt out of the Ambulance ready to run for home when his eyes caught the sight of that wildly hairy ginger, walking out from the bushes towards the warehouse.

It was Brandon.

Something felt strange to Joe and it wasn't the newly found strength his bowel had discovered, now pushing his once compactified matter back up like a raging river crashing against a dam that was his struggling sphincter.

Joe knew Brandon would meet at this location in

case of emergencies, however the mere sight of Brandon brought uncontrollable tears to Joe's unsuspecting tear ducts, as he subconsciously mourned a loss he never knew.

"Brandon! Stop…", yelled Joe, not wanting his best friend to get caught up with the strange man who was walking up to the hole in the fence. The very same hole that only Brandon and Joe were meant to know about.

"Oi! Is this pervert trying to abduct you?", Brandon bellowed, deepening his boyish voice in an effort to intimidate the strange man as he walked up to Joe near the rear of the Ambulance, peering inside and half expecting to see the bodies of several kidnapped children.

"Why the hell are you crying dude? Seriously, who is this guy?" Brandon stood back, looking at Joe's blood-stained clothes and back at the strange man who was now through the fence line and walking into the warehouse, his wonderous mullet wig waving in the wind as his short stumpy legs carried his disproportionate upper torso through the long grass.

The peculiar sensation of nostalgia passed, and Joe was able to think straight again. "No, I don't think he's any trouble. He came to my house after things got a little crazy, I don't know where to begin man..."

"You can begin by coming over here!", shouted the strange man, popping his head out of the warehouse entrance.

"Dude, I'm not getting chopped up into cat food for some weird guy with a mullet, just so he can wear my skin over his face while he dresses up like a woman on a Wednesday night", Brandon exclaimed, with a little too much detail. Joe scrunched up his brow and narrowed his eyes at Brandon ready to berate him, when another wave of nostalgia hit him instead.

Grabbing onto Brandon's arm as he fell to one knee, Joe heard his blood curdling screams echo through his memories.

"Woah, this isn't cool, you are starting to freak me out man", Brandon told Joe, pulling him to his feet and patting his back with all the sympathy that an ice-cream vendor gives to a lactose intolerant customer.

Depending on what side of the counter you're on, that could be a lot of sympathy, or none at all. I'm going to leave that analogy open to interpretation. Hey, live a little! I can't give you all the answers.

As if in tune with Joe's inner voices, the strange man popped his head back out from behind the warehouse entrance and yelled, "If you want all those weird memories and Deja Vu's to make any kind of sense, you need to come in here and see this for yourself", before disappearing again into the shadows.

Joe had to know. He needed to know. Joe knew how bad not knowing was, now knowing that the strange man knew what he wanted to know without knowing that he knew. You know what I mean. Wait...haven't we done this before? Talk about lazy writing.

"I think he's right man, it's alright if you don't wanna come, but I need to know", Joe said, puffing his chest out and marching towards the hole in the fence with as much purpose as a porpoise, purposely perusing a preposterous penguin doing a pole dance.

"Uh uh, I'm coming with you dude. It beats poking dead whale carcasses with a stick!", Brandon said with restrained enthusiasm, running over to Joe and giving him a wide grin that barely hid his own anxiety.

Each step drew Joe closer to the front door of the warehouse, with its large black iron doors mangled on either side, twisted and warped from a fire that stripped it down to its basic masonry and steel pillars almost ten years ago. Without warning, the strange man popped back out through the front door, but this time wearing a white lab coat, black business pants, thick reading glasses and a blonde comb over toupee that had seen better days.

"What the hell man!", Joe yelled as he jumped backwards, losing his patience with this obscure man and his lack of explanations.

"Ah yeah, about that... I'll explain everything in due course boy. Nice to see you again Brandon, glad you could come", said the strange man, with an exuberant amount of confidence in his well-rehearsed words.

Brandon stopped meters from the door and shouted at the strange man, "You even think of asking me to play 'Tickle Tickle, lets hide the pickle' and I'll cut it off! I'm warning you!"

The strange man didn't even register the threat, disappearing into the blackness of the warehouse once more.

With one last blank look at each other and with a unified shrug of the shoulders, Joe and Brandon stepped two a breast into the void.

Bang!

If smells had a sound it would be just that. It hit the olfactory senses of Joe and Brandon's brain like a forty-calibre hollow point bullet of stench to the temple.

"Mother of god, what is that smell?", Brandon gagged, putting his right arm across his nose and mouth as his eyes watered.

Joe froze as the strange man stood in front of them with his hands respectively by his side and a pile of rusted metal heaped behind him. "This isn't easy to say, but behind me is a dead Brandon"

"Oh, hell no! My face is way too pretty to become your mask SICKO!", Brandon screamed, pulling out his small swiss army knife and pointing the teaspoon menacingly at the strange man. "Let's get out of here Joe...JOE!"

Joe walked forward in a hypnotic trance towards the metal pile, the smell of putrefaction not affecting his judgement in the slightest. The strange man stepped aside and bowed his head in another respectful gesture. Joe couldn't help but feel he was being genuine.

Emerging from the large pile of crushed and corroded metal were two white shoes sticking upwards attached to two very slimy tibia bones. On closer inspection, Joe could see the remainder of the decomposing human carcass intertwined in the metal, with maggots and beetles working their networks in and out of the fleshy stew.

"Dude we gotta get out of here, it's some kind of sick prank", Brandon stammered, arms shaking under the surge of adrenaline as he held onto the spoon for dear life, ready to disembowel the strange man one tiny scoop at a time.

"Brandon…I'm sorry, but it's true", Joe turned to Brandon with a single tear running down his cheek and a white shoe in his hand. "Look, it has your name written on the tongue in your hand writing, it's the same shoe's you have on right now! I remember something happening here, I don't know how or why but this was you".

Brandon dropped the spoon, walking forwards like a Catholic priest who just sighted a fresh batch of altar boys. "Let me see…I have to see"

"Ah I can't let you do that boy", the strange man stood in-between Joe and Brandon, both arms outstretched pushing against each of the boy's chests with force that implied he was serious.

"Let's all sit down, and I'll talk you through this", he said, pointing to three milk crates situated nearby on the dusty floor, "Just don't let Brandon near that shoe, ok?"

"Um, ok", Joe replied meekly, pulling the shoe close to his chest while Brandon sceptically squinted his eyes back at the metal heap, as he walked to the milk crates, hoping to see further proof of his deceased other self.

"Firstly", Brandon pouted as he sat down, "This is the dumbest hoax of all Joe. Nice try with the water works, but how am I meant to believe that's me over there when I'm sitting right here!"

"Let me answer that boy", the strange man sharply retorted, taking off his overly thick reading glasses and rubbing his eyes impatiently.

"Alright then. But before we do this, what's your name? Because calling you, 'The Strange Man', is just confusing for everyone", quipped Joe, breaking the fourth wall to the reader which is supposed to be the narrator's job...Thanks Joe.

"Bob...you can call me Bob", said Bob, ruining any build up I may have been hoping to create...Thanks Bob.

•

INTERMISSION

Put on some standard elevator music, turn the lights down low and take a trip to the Candy Bar of Knowledge before you embark on the next part of the book.

Unfortunately, the bar is all out of 'Scientifically Accurate' snacks, but feel free to grab a one litre bottle of 'Semi-Correct Statements', a large popcorn drizzled in non-dairy 'Fiction', and top it off with my favourite ice cream flavour, the 'This-isn't-how-physics-works' sundae.

All set? Good.

•

"The town you live in, Doomsville, is encased in a time-bubble", Bob began, gesturing his hands with as much enthusiasm as a semi-retired Chemistry teacher.

"This bubble is situated perfectly around Doomsville. Its boundaries lie just outside the fence line, seemingly on purpose. The time-bubble has been locked onto this particular day, repeating it for the past three years and resetting itself at midnight. Everyone trapped inside the bubble is reset. Bodies, memories and all."

"Pfft whatever man, you should be

institutionalized", Brandon scoffed, looking at Joe expecting the same response, but instead finding an enthralled child-like boy staring at Bob with wide eyes as if he had learned the meaning of life.

"Yeah, yeah. I know", Bob rubbed the bridge of his nose in an irritated manner.

"Trust me Brandon, this isn't the first time we've had this talk. Now don't make me go through the whole 'How many fingers am I holding up', or 'What am I going to say next' routine, because frankly I'm over it! Instead, if you interrupt me again, I'll just tell Joe here your most embarrassing story"

"Ha…", Brandon replied timidly, unsure of where to go next, but too cocky to back down. "Go ahead man, you don't know me"

Bob flew into the story as if it was a well-known fairy tale etched into his memory.

"It was last winter, or should I say, the last winter you can remember. Your second cousin Maria was visiting from France with the entire cast of the Doomsville Circus…"

"No way…"

"…it wasn't necessarily the Donkey that caught your attention…"

"Dude, ok stop…"

"…but when you saw the bearded lady and the world's strongest dwarf behind the tent with Maria…"

"OK! Holy crap man!", hands on top of his head as if he'd just had a brain enema, Brandon was shaken to the core. Joe appeared more confused than a child being accidently shown a video of their birth in reverse.

"ummm….so how many times have you had to tell us this?", Brandon quietly whispered to Bob, face flush red in embarrassment.

"Too many times boy, too many…", Bob stood up and grabbed the shoe from Joe and pointed at Brandon. "Take your shoe off and throw it in the middle of the room"

Without a single complaint and not wanting any further divulsion of that one strange encounter being released publicly, Brandon ripped his shoe off faster than you could say, "Circus Meat Sandwich". Sorry Brandon, I couldn't help myself.

"So, this version of Brandon behind us was killed approximately one month ago by a man who goes by the name, *The Master*", Bob voiced out loud while pacing the circle of milk crates. "However, this Brandon died outside the time-bubble, that's why your rotting corpse didn't disappear from here and is still stinking the place out"

"Why does this all sound familiar?", Joe asked, clinging to the edge of his crate like an eagle on its perch, ready to take this psychological dive into the unknown.

"Ah well boy, you're getting ahead of yourself a little. Let me finish this part first", Bob said, waving his hand dismissively in Joe's direction, but at the same time easing his feeling of apprehension with a gentle wink.

"You were here too when you both fought valiantly against *The Master's* creation, a terrible Dumpster of Doom"

"That Master bastard", Brandon said with no real conviction, still unsure whether to commit fully to this crazed idea or pretend to agree in order to save his shredded dignity.

"You faced the Dumpster again later that day Joe, this time you single handily defeated *The Master's* creation at the Rubbish Dump. The day reset at midnight and so did Brandon, with no memory of his gruesome death"

Brandon looked sheepishly over at the pile of metal and flesh that was once a previous version of himself and shuddered.

"Unfortunately, *The Master* found a way to melt down its defeated creation and reanimate the new monster who attacked you today Joe", Bob continued.

"Wait, wait, wait!", Joe pushed himself up slowly from his seat and extended his index finger at Bob. "My parents died only three days ago! You said this Dumpster attacked us last month...I don't understand"

"Ahh yes boy, I know it's a hard concept to grasp", Bob hung his head low. "To you, your parents dying feels like three days ago. But trust me, it has been more like three years...You've relived the same day with the same memories ever since then"

"But...but...", Joe sat back down on the crate with a thud as his arms flopped between his gangly legs, his brain on fire as it fought to comprehend this life altering revelation. "You say my parents died three years ago...and the time-bubble has been up for about three years...is that a coincidence?"

"Stay with me now Joe", Bob implored emphatically. "I don't know much else about why the time-bubble occurred, but there were rumours of *The Master* fleeing from your house on the night your parents died. Three days later...Boom! The time-bubble went up"

Joe's mouth opened and closed like a laughing clown arcade game at the local Carnival.

"I've lived outside of the time-bubble ever since that fateful day, watching *The Master* from afar and sometimes up close, hence my cunning disguises", Bob said proudly, "I've foiled any plans I could, and I've been successful for some time. But *The Master's* inventions are now beyond my capabilities and I knew it was time to bring you both in on this"

Bob turned his mighty pectorals to face Brandon, "And yes, you'll play your part too boy. You'll need to help keep Joe safe until the time is right". Brandon sat quiet, biting his bottom lip nervously and looking over at Joe.

"I injected you with a serum today Joe, which will slowly bring back your quantum state memories. You're probably feeling the effects already. I'll show you both how to administer your own serum and teach you how to live inside the time-bubble without losing your memories"

Bob stood back up, his hands clenched with a newly found energy and his blonde toupee comb-over standing upright at attention. "That's how we will take the advantage back from *The Master*. He will never suspect that we know the truth. And us knowing that he doesn't know...", Bob droned on and on. I mean, how many 'knowing' puns do you think we can get away with in one book?

"The Dumpster and Toaster...they weren't the first things to attack me, were they?", Joe questioned.

"Not at all boy. I made a long list of all the inventions *The Master* made before the Dumpster. Most failed spectacularly, but as his powers grew his ability to influence more and more complicated artificial systems increased. And for a man who has the day on repeat, time is literally on his side", Bob replied, grabbing the shoe from Joe's hands and holding it up in the air.

"Watch this Brandon", he said as he threw it toward the other shoe in the middle of the circle.

As if the shoes were made of liquid, they both merged into one and began to shrink before their very eyes, erupting in a powerful sonic boom and throwing the boys off their milk crates. The result was a small but powerful cylindrical beam of energy from floor to roof.

All that was left in the aftermath, was a burnt circular mark on the concrete floor and a hole in the tin roof.

"Holy f...physics man", Brandon yelled out extatically, forcing the narrator to censor his foul mouth.

"You see, on a quantum level, no two identical objects can co-exist in the same space at the same time. Being near each other caused that paradox you just saw. So, if you're ever outside of the time-bubble when it resets, don't go giving yourself a nice hug when you re-enter", said Bob, sitting back down on his milk crate as if nothing had happened, while Joe and Brandon watched standing in awe, trying not to squeal like excitable turkeys on the eve of Thanksgiving dinner.

"B-bob", Joe stuttered, barely able to contain himself, "So why me? Why was *The Master* there when my parents died? And how does *The Master* create these monsters?"

"Hmm", Bob thought, not wanting to drown the reader in too much information in one sitting, thinking of the best way to slowly release it in vague but meaningful ways and not wanting to receive the full rapture of the narrator should he fail to stick to the plan. No pressure Bob.

"We need to travel back into town. I need to show you something in the Library about *The Master* before it gets too dark. We can talk more about it after that", reassured Bob, keeping to the agreed storyline like a good little boy.

Chapter Six

And Then a Step to the Right...

The Treacherous Tyrant of Trauma and his Toaster of Terror, tenaciously toiled trial after trial, the many tasteless ways to torture and totally terrify the townspeople, all of whom are trapped in a timeless loop of terminal tragedy.

Barbaric as it may be to brutally break open our bold and bodacious hero's skull, before belligerently bottling his brain, this Bloodthirsty Bohemian of Butchery truly believes this act will baptize himself of his besieged and bereaved past.

•

Prior to leaving the warehouse grounds, Bob reminded Joe and Brandon of the significance of this newly bestowed knowledge.

"Whatever you do, whoever you come across back in town, don't divulge the truth to them. Even if you're captured by *The Master* himself and tortured in unspeakable, unimaginable, inhumane and downright confusing ways...say nothing", Bob paused for dramatic effect, looking upwards in the distance with his right hand grasping his dimpled chin, overacting his part of the concerned vigilante.

Brandon and Joe exchanged cringed looks at one another and set off to the fence line without Bob, who assured them he would meet them in the town's library alone.

Not a word was spoken between Joe and Brandon as they trudged through the empty streets of Doomsville side by side, heads bowed down with a dark cloud of melancholy hanging over them as the realization of their fake reality seeped through to the core of their overflowing cerebrums.

After fighting a feral cat who'd claimed one of Aileen's stray eyeballs as a trophy, Joe looked up as they neared the towns central park. Standing in the middle, encased in black jagged metal was the Doomsville clock.

3:46pm.

"Shit!", Joe let go of Aileen's optic nerve that he and the overweight cat had been playing tug of war with, sending the feline flying. "We don't have much time man, the Library closes soon. We gotta pick up the pace."

"Yeah, but don't run dude", Brandon whispered, looking around like the anonymous farter in a crowded elevator, "We don't know who *The Master* has as spies around here"

Quickening their pace so it resembled more of a power walker holding in explosive diarrhea, Joe and Brandon reached the large double doors of the library located opposite the small police station, catching the glares of the dozen or so citizens taking a Saturday afternoon stroll through the town's park. Wait! So there ARE citizens in Doomsville? Here I was thinking the author was just being incompetent...

Once inside the safety of the Library, the musky air that smells like the urine stained carpet at a retirement village, attacked their delicate nostrils, causing Brandon to dry reach. The interior of the Library was small but cosy, with tall mahogany bookshelves scattered sporadically, a singular wooden table in the middle of the room covered with unorganised index cards and a broken microfilm reader in a corner.

"Shhhh!", came a warning from behind Joe and Brandon, so sharp it pierced their eardrums in several different wavelengths. Jumping a full one hundred and eighty degrees, Joe Judo chopped the air like a chromosome impaired stick insect, while Brandon opted to use one hand to shield his face and the other to protect his small but sensitive manhood.

"Uh guys, it's me", whispered Bob who was wearing a long grey wig tied in a tight bun, small semi-circle reading glasses chained around his neck, a nice little yellow and blue floral dress, and rocking six-inch heels which displayed his somewhat hairless and well-defined calves perfectly. I mean, God damn Bob! What are your plans after this Chapter?...

"Woah dude", said Brandon, deepening his voice and puffing out his chest like an insecure squirrel who grabbed the wrong set of nuts...if you catch my drift. "What's with the goofy getup? We can totally tell it's you, you're not fooling anyone"

"Hmm interesting", Bob smiled deviously as he pulled at his groin in a very un-lady like manner, trying to prevent the loss of all lower body circulation as his two-sizes-too-small pantyhose threatened to engulf him like a sexy boa constrictor.

Locking the Library's entry door behind him, Bob wiggled his hips back to the boys who didn't quite know how to react, both looking awkwardly to the ground and up to the ceiling in alternating turns.

"You certainly haven't recognized me in this Library before Brandon, especially with those over-due books. Let's see, ah yes there was that one from the

'Teen Puberty 'section and another from the 'Home Cooking' section. Both had pages missing in area's which leaves even me concerned", Bob jeered out loud, pulling his reading glasses down his nose like a true librarian. "Then there was that time you actually asked me out on a date! It's ok, I understand. Growing up as a teenager can have its confusing stages"

"Oh, come on man!", Brandon whimpered, looking at Joe and back to Bob seeking mercy. "I've had enough embarrassment for one day, let's just get on with it"

"Sure thing, but remember young boy, my eyes are up here!", Bob jested, pushing past the boys and walking to the centre of the room, taking a seat on a stool by the table with as much elegance as a pig in a tutu performing Swan Lake.

Joe squinted at Brandon shaking his head with bemusement as Brandon pretended to look away, both taking a seat opposite Bob with the sinister lighting of several candles on tall poles filling the room with an overwhelming sense of foreboding.

Sure, there are electrical lights in the Library, but who waits to the second Part of the book for a major twist to be revealed under artificial light. Uncultured mood wrecker!

"Alright Bob, we're here now. Tell us what you know of *The Master*", Joe said feverishly, his legs jigging uncontrollably as he hungered for the truth.

"Good, good", Bob clapped his hands together, "what I can show you here is the chain of events in Doomsville which I believe *The Master* was behind, resulting in your parent's death Joe and our time-bubble predicament. I can also tell you the source of his power..."

Like a magician with a bottomless hat, Bob fumbled in his well-padded bra and pulled out a large manila folder, slamming it on the table with one hairy hand on top, glancing at Joe for a moment, then tilting his head slowly to Brandon before looking back down at his hand.

"Are you both in? Once we start down this path, there's no turning back", Bob emphasized every syllable, "We've never gotten this far before. I'm afraid we might not get another chance". A sadness crept into his voice as he closed his eyes, preparing himself for the same rejection he had experienced many time-loops before.

Joe placed his small clammy hands on top of Bob's before glaring at Brandon, who without a second's notice slammed his freckled hand on top with more confidence than a Japanese whale harpooner, searching for his morbidly obese bride.

"Alright!" Bob threw his hand up ecstatically almost flinging the boys off their stools, grinning like a madman.

"Let's look at this chronologically…", Bob said as he opened the folder with care.

"According to the Doom Times Newspaper article in 1985, there was a cinema ban put in place", Bob pulled a movie ticket out from the folder. "If it were really banned it'd be impossible for me to have this"

DOOMSVILLE THEATRE, 20/01/2009, CHICKENS: A PECK TOO FAR Seat 3 Isle B

"Dude, what kind of movies were you watching?", Brandon jeered, catching himself mid-laugh as he saw the seriousness in Joe's eyes.

Bob pulled the ticket away and placed it down his bra, visibly hurt by the comment, "It wasn't mine…it was my sons"

"Is he still…alive?", Joe questioned, not sure he wanted to know the answer.

"The strange thing about this time-bubble is that once it was turned on, everyone I ever knew is neither dead or alive", Bob retorted, not really answering the question but getting 9 out of 10 for mysteriousness.

"But that's not all", Bob re-adjusted himself, pulling paper article after paper article from the folder, showing the banning of school books on physics in 1992, the boundary fence line being erected in 1998, the technology ban of 2008, and many, many more.

"All these were pivotal points in time for Doomsville, adjusted on purpose to isolate and control this town. *The Master* re-wrote our history one page at time", Bob leant back, exhausted.

Joe and Brandon examined each article closely along with contradictory articles from Bob's previous timeline, proving his theory and going into further detail which would ordinarily bore the general slack jawed audience and therefore has been stricken from the Chapter. Thank me later.

"Ha!", Brandon lifted up an article attempting to poke a metaphorical hole in Bob's conspiracy. "Why would anyone bother travelling back in time to ban two and three ply toilet paper? That's not world dominating stuff there!"

"It's rather ingenious, you just need to think outside the box", Bob winked at Joe, sensing another opportunity to ridicule Brandon.

"Removing two and three ply toilet paper altogether forced the masses to use one ply paper like SAVAGES!" Bob brought both his apelike hands down onto the table with immense force, closing his eyes in pain as he recalled the horrifically smelly one ply memories.

"Being too thin to work effectively, it resulted in some…sticky situations. This was used to fuel fear about rising Hepatitis E levels due to the lack of cleanliness, forcing the population the vaccinate. However, the 'vaccine' was not a vaccine at all, but instead was a drug to help brainwash the masses so they wouldn't notice the timeline changes *The Master* was making." Bob finished his statement with more smugness than Smuggy the smuggler, who smuggled smugly. That's pretty smug.

"Oh…wow", Brandon lowered his arms, feeling overwhelmed by the complexity of the situation.

"Ok then, how come this guy didn't just travel back further in time and make himself ruler of the country, or the world! For someone with the ability to time travel, this seems like a ridiculous way to use it", Brandon questioned, screwing up his nose as if he were Einstein reborn.

"All I know about his time travel ability, is that he had every intention of ruling the world. That was until the fateful night Joe's parents died. Whatever he did that night caused major issues to his time travelling plans, forcing him to lock this day down and find what he needed to fix it…", said Bob, sitting forward on his stool resting his elbows on the table, clasping his meaty hands together so hard his knuckles turned white and intentionally avoiding the discussion of Joe's brain.

Conveniently not listening to that plot spoiler, Joe spread the articles out on the table, excitedly pointing to a cloaked figure found in the background of each photo, all with an unusually bulbous shaped head hidden under a hood. "Wait! In all these pictures there's the same guy. Is this *The Master*?"

"Yes, good work boy. He's been working hard in the shadows, influencing where he could to build his evil empire…until he met you", Bob pulled out the last article of the folder and held it up high, sighing deeper than a 1970's soul singer.

"Now you know what he's changed in the past. Its time you know how he does it", Bob continued, before being interrupted by a much-needed Segue.

•

Approaching Roxanne's family residence like an elderly lion with no teeth, *The Master* tucked his creation under his arm and strutted through the extensively landscaped pathway leading up to the mansion, carrying with him all the confidence of a janitor walking into a portable toilet after a large concert at a cheese and wine festival.

"I wonder my marvellous machine, will they accommodate us for dinner?", cackled *The Master*, stroking his metallic hands on the surface of the Toaster as electric sparks arched between the two like some forbidden love taboo.

"I WILL ACCOMMODATE...THEIR BRAINS!", screeched the annoying homeware device, making a completely nonsensical yet disturbing threat that only a dim-witted-

SLAP

Ouch!

'Ok, ok', said the narrator rubbing his cheek, as *The Master* of mediocre somehow breached all novel writing ethics and physical constraints, to slap me with the strength of a fasting vegetarian.

"Don't think I can't hear you, you pompous, fat, floating head of a narrator. You better change your tune!", said the marvellous and magnificent Master of mayhem.

"That's better", *The Master* remarked.

He knocked on the front door with a wrist so limp, it makes an impotent fish seem invigorated-

-"Hey stop that!", snarled Master McSnarly at the narrators witty and charming humour.

"I'm warning you…Frank!"

Ahh, using first names are we? You must be serious. Alright, let's give this another go then. If you want flattery, I'll give you flattery.

With more man than mandible, this fine specimen of testosterone rapped upon Roxanne's front door with so much vigour and potency, he impregnated the surrounding eco-system with his rhythmic knocks.

"What in the hell are you on about?", questioned *The Master* of my dreams.

Oh, so you don't like that hey? There simply is no pleasing you!

"Argh!" screwing up his metal hands into fists and shaking them at the sky, *The Master* admits defeat. "FINE! Just narrate in your usual, boring fashion. It doesn't matter to me. For at the end of this book, it is I that will be victor-"

The door opened as *The Master* of midway sentences was caught out…midway.

A tall British stereotype opened the door. It was Roxanne's father, Cornelius Beige.

"Um, excuse me Sir, but what the devil are you doing rambling to yourself on my front door?"

The Master looked around, his annoyingly large cranium swaying from side to side like an over-inflated breast implant.

"Ah good man, we are here for supper. But I guess we should have booked...A HEAD!", screamed *The Master*, releasing his grip on the glorified metal paperweight he called a toaster, which fired two razor sharp pieces of toast at Cornelius.

The first piece sliced clean through his jugular at a ninety-degree angle, embedding itself in the door frame behind his head. The second piece skimmed the scalp, cutting through the top of Cornelius's skull and exposing his pink fleshy brain.

Cornelius fell to his knees in slow motion, chocking on the torrents of blood flooding his lungs from the cut arterial line.

The impact of his knees hitting the ground sent a shockwave up through his body and into his open cranium. His unprotected brain shot upwards through the top of his skull, making a popping noise not too dissimilar to the sound of someone sucking out that last bit of meat from a cooked crab claw.

The Master gave the narrator one last look of cold

indifference before entering the front hallway of the Beige residence with his metallic monster in tow. The screams of the desperate Beige family echoed into the night as *The Master* makes a murderous point about being taken seriously.

Point taken you masochistic Master...Point taken.

Chapter Seven
Don't Pay the Ferryman

Welcome back. Changed your underpants? I know I have.

Before we get back to the last of Bob's boring, yet contextually important discussion, let's just cover some plot holes I know you're going to ask, but I have no intention of explaining:

1)   Why couldn't Bob just show the boys the folder of articles in the warehouse? Did he really have to dress up like a very attractive librarian and unnecessarily risk their lives by making them return to the centre of town?

2)   How can a movie ticket from the previous timeline exist inside the time-bubble which erased that event in the past? Paradox anyone?

3)   Why a dumpster? Why a toaster? Couldn't *The Master* just melt them down into a gun? Bang! Book finished at page 2! A child could have written this...

Now, this book is like a Paralympian with no arms competing in a Triathlon.

The first leg of the race was fast and easy with a one-hundred-meter sprint. No problems there.

The second leg is the swimming stage of the race, which is a bit of a struggle, but you managed to push through.

The final leg is white water rafting. This is where you lose all direction and control and wonder, "Why the hell am I doing this? I HAVE NO ARMS!"

So, with that in mind, lets wade into this final leg of the race, albeit in a proverbial brown creek of effluent without a paddle, because you still have no arms. Together we will push through to the other side where murderous appliances and good times continue. See what I did there?

•

MEANWHILE BACK AT THE LIBRARY

"And that's where his power comes from", Bob finished his explanation prematurely, stretching his arms above his head.

I should acknowledge that time in this book is linear page to page. Bob was most likely explaining the important details while we broke off for that Segue. Sorry guys, rookie narrator mistake.

"Ahh, that makes so much sense now, it's almost like there's no mystery to it anymore", gloated

Brandon, rubbing it in your face.

"Yeah man! So, a meteorite crashed just outside Doomsville and was transported to the abandoned warehouse. *The Master* somehow got a hold of it, hid it and now uses its power for himself. And it's called Doomite? That's easy to remember", reiterated Joe, who deserves a gold star for that back capture of detail.

"Exactly, you guys are fast learners", a relieved Bob exhaled, freed from his burden of knowledge and happy to no longer be alone in this loopy looped time.

"He must have transported it down those super accessible mine-shafts just outside the fence line. That means…", Joe trailed off in deep thought as Brandon's telepathy for the obvious kicked in.

"…that he moved it to the epi-centre of Doomsville, the abandoned mine under the town park!", exclaimed Brandon, as chuffed with himself as a winner of a spelling bee contest, who refused to acknowledge that all the other contestants had severe speech impediments.

"I'm ready to take this bastard down! Turns out he doesn't have some scary voodoo magic at all. Probably just some stolen Alien technology!", touted Joe, kicking his stool back like a drunken donkey as he stood up with fists clenched, ready to punch fate in the face.

Aliens hey? Hold onto that thought. Wink wink. Nudge nudge.

"That's our plan then boys. First, we need to get back to my caravan. I need to make sure you can survive in the time-bubble with your memories intact. It's imperative to our survival-", Bob's speech was cut off mid-sentence by the sound of the old public telephone ringing on the library reception desk.

Bob gingerly stood up from his seat and pulled the mightiest wedgie out from his panty-hose which was buried deeper than the food he had for lunch.

"Hello, Doomsville library, how can I help you my dear?", Bob's gruff impersonation of an elderly woman sounded more like a throat cancer survivor, gargling through their tracheotomy, leaving Joe and Brandon perplexed as to how he stayed undetected for so long.

Bob slowly put the receiver on the counter and turned to Joe with a look of deep empathy, before mouthing, 'It's for you'.

Joe walked over and collected the receiver, immediately feeling the warmth from his body disappear.

"JOE HELP ME! YOU HAVE TO HELP-"

Roxanne. Sweet, innocent, only friends and not quiet official girlfriend of Joe and probably never will be at this rate, especially if he doesn't save her again, Roxanne.

"Roxanne! Hello? Hello?!", Joe gripped the phone receiver with both hands, strangling its poor little receiver neck until it cracked in the middle. What did the phone ever do to you Joe? Haven't enough things died already!

"...Hello there Joe, I hope you can join Roxy and I for dinner", came the shrill voice of *The Master* on the other end of the not yet dead, but critically injured phone receiver.

"You dare touch her...", Joe began his cliché white male protagonist speech.

"My, my. I wouldn't dream of it my child. But my creation you met earlier...well, let's just say he has a way of getting in peoples...HEADS! Ha! You have fifteen minutes, don't leave the Beige family waiting...", and with that *The Master* hung up.

In a rage of small proportions, Joe stomped to the door like an irate frill necked lizard on a cold day.

"Woah now boy, ease up there", Bob placed his

banana-bunched hands on Joe's chest pushing him back, yet still holding that empathetic glare, a glare Joe recognized deep down but couldn't quite place.

"We need to get back to my caravan, it's getting late and we need to prepare for the reset at midnight", Bob pleaded as Brandon slapped his hand on Joe's shoulder from behind in a comforting gesture.

"Dude, the day will reset and whatever happens to her tonight will be like it never happened. She won't remember. Sounds horrible man, but it makes sense to go back with Bob", Brandon walked around to face Joe who refused to look him in the eyes, tears of anger and pain building up behind his black eyes as he looked out the Library's front glass doors.

If we could freeze this frame it would be indicative of one of those B-grade 1990's boyband music videos, full of contradictory heterosexual homoeroticism. Say that to your Grandmother three times.

"I'm not that kind of person! She shouldn't have to suffer, no matter what the circumstances, no matter what the timeline!", yelled Joe through gritted teeth as he squeezed past Bob and Brandon, pushing the glass doors open with both hands, watching the sun set slowly over Rubbish Dump Ridge. Joe paused for a moment, taking a deep breath in to help quell his rage.

"Please boy", Bob implored, his voice shaking now as he walked up to Joe, both standing side by side and looking outwards from the library. "It took me...", Bob cut himself off as Joe looked over to Bob who pulled a notepad out of...somewhere? I mean, he doesn't have pockets and those panty-hose are super tight, so it's probably best we don't know.

"...967 attempts to get you this far. Please, don't go." Bob stepped back, giving Joe room to think and concealing that notepad God knows where.

"Thank you for what you've done, really I mean it. But I'm not you, and I need to do this", Joe softened his voice, turning to Brandon, "Are you coming man?"

Brandon sighed heavily, "Jesus dude, alright. You're gonna get me killed...again!"

Bob stopped Brandon as he exited the Library, "Do whatever you have to, but just get Joe back to my caravan, ok? He's the key to all of this. Here's a map to my location once you've finished. You must get back there before midnight."

With his hands shaking worse than an emotionally abused jackhammer, Brandon accepted the map and placed it in his small emergency backpack.

"You're not coming?", Brandon asked, still not quite sure how to take the librarian disguise which was bringing back all kinds of very confusing memories, possibly scarring him for life.

"No boy, I watch. It's what I do. I interfered at the Rubbish Dump which almost got me caught. If *The Master* catches me before I have trained you both, then we're all doomed. Good luck boys", and with that Bob walked off into the darkness at the other end of the library, only the clicking of his six-inch heels could be heard as he walked away.

Without looking back, Joe broke into a sprint down the street with Brandon in tow.

"We...got...a...plan...bro?", Brandon panted, his freckled cheeks flushing redder than a baboon's rear during mating season.

"Save Roxanne. Plan later", Joe spurted back, his lungs were on fire, his legs were jelly, his arms felt like lead and they had only made it twenty meters up the road.

Several short stops later, Joe and Brandon made it to the snobby estate which housed Roxanne's parent's mansion, located on the opposite side of town to Joe's run-down neighbourhood. Large swaths of pristine landscaped gardens, stables, orchards and manors filled this estate. Almost all were government employee's, which now had Joe questioning how close they were to *The Master* and what kind of roles they had all played to allow themselves such fine seats at his table of death.

Slowing their approach to the front of her house, they could see the door was wide open with bloodied drag marks trailing from outside the house into the hallway. Peeking through the window near the door, Brandon could see a fire was lit in the lounge room with a singular black leather chair in front. Beyond that he could see the dining room door was open, letting soft light emanate outwards.

"What do you see?", Joe whispered, keeping an eye on the front door and searching for any makeshift weapons in the garden.

"I can see the dining room and the lounge room, the rest of the house is in darkness. There're a few people sitting at a dining table and a seat in the lounge room near a fire. What do you wanna do man?", Brandon whispered back, crouching under the windowsill.

"JOE! HELLLLP...", Roxanne's voice bellowed out through the front door. Joe looked down at his watch.

7:13pm.

It was now or never.

Come to think of it, in this time-loop the term 'now' means today, yesterday and tomorrow. Tomorrows yesterday and yesterday's tomorrow is also today. So, technically for Joe now is infinite, so its infinite or never. But if he chooses never, it's still infinite. So, its infinite or infinite. Wait, what?... never mind.

Joe glanced at Brandon who was now frantically searching the rose bushes, throwing Joe a small gardening trowel as he wielded his own mighty miniaturized rake.

You've heard of the brave soldiers that stormed the beaches in World War II? Well this was nothing like that. Joe and Brandon ran into the open entrance with the fury of an angry waddle of miniature penguins.

"OHHH SHITTT!!!", howled Brandon after he turned the corner from the hallway into the lounge room's doorway.

Joe stopped in his tracks and watched a piece of toast fly directly at him from out of the dark, cutting his cheek above his jawline and slicing up under his left eye, spraying the wall in a thin layer of fresh blood.

Turning around, Joe saw Brandon was pinned to the

lounge room doorframe with a large piece of sharpened toast stuck deep in his left trapezium muscle, just above the shoulder. The piece of toast was holding Brandon's body inches off the floor as he kicked his legs furiously in the air.

"Leave him there my child. Unless of course you want him to be...CUT DOWN TO SIZE! Ha haa", came a voice behind the large leather seat facing the fire at the far end of the room. A large silhouette of an abnormally round head flickered across the ceiling. Joe would have to cover at least ten meters to get close. He had to make a choice.

"You bastard. You call yourself *The Master* but you're just a coward", Joe spat towards the figure, who remained motionless in the chair.

"Manners, manners. How about you make your way to the dining room. The Beige family are...DYING to meet you!", squeaked *The Master* as he reached the end of his badly executed pun.

Joe pivoted on the spot, hopelessly searching for the direction the piece of toast had come from, unsure whether to take on *The Master* himself.

"Time is ticking my child, don't make me lose my patience", hissed *The Master*, clicking his metallic fingers, causing another scream to ring out from the dining room.

"Go man… save her", urged Brandon, withering in pain against the wall as he placed his hands on the hardened piece of toast, trying to relieve the pressure.

"I'll come back for you", said Joe, walking towards the dining room only meters away, keeping his peripherals locked on the leather seat, expecting a sneak attack.

Slow drawn-out violins played through surround sound speakers in every corner of the open planned black and white dining room. The lights were dimmed down to only a fraction of their potential. As Joe neared the end of the large wooden dining table, he could only just make out the outline of three people seated.

To the left of Joe sat an elderly lady, wearing an elegant blue evening gown with a large pearl necklace emphasizing her white hair. A young male with black sleek hair matching his tuxedo, sat on the other side of the table. At the head of the table sat an older male with streaks of grey through his well-groomed hair, set against his three buttoned blue suit.

Hang on, let me get this straight? The author describes three strangers better than he has described the main character in over one hundred pages? He's as consistent as a Taco Tuesday fart...

Joe moved closer to the end of the table, moving his gaze from one person to the next, concentrating harder than an orange who's getting squeezed for its concentrate, while it concentrated on passing a concentration test.

"Mr. Beige? Mrs. Beige?", Joe whispered, extending his freed hand out to the elderly lady seated next to him, his fingers only inches away from touching her shoulder, doing all the things you shouldn't do in a creepy dark house where the villain has given you way too many ominous hints.

Blinding light filled in the room as the dimmers were suddenly turned up to maximum output, burning Joe's retina's back to their evolutionary origins, making the one time he contracted a super resistant strain of 'Pink eye' from Aileen's controversial pea and ham soup, seem like a minor irritation in comparison.

Shielding his eyes with one arm, Joe took a step back from the table and swung the trowel from left to right in an automatic response to the fear building up inside his small fragile body. Peeking steadily above his arm, Joe's eyes adjusted to the light, allowing him to absorb the magnitude of the situation.

All three Beige members had generous amounts of silver duct tape wrapped around their torso's and foreheads, securing them to their chairs and keeping them seated upright. Their gaunt pale faces showed no sign of life, only a frozen contorted look of anguish, giving Joe a terrifying insight into their final moments.

The deep red blood which had soaked into the front of their garments was now coagulating in large chunks, much like Aileen's pea and ham soup. It's the analogy that keeps on giving.

Their necks had been sliced open so deep Joe could see the cartilage between each victims vertebras. A line of fishing wire trailed from the top of their heads up to the ceiling and through a pulley system, before trailing back down to the kitchen area at the far end of the room. Cautiously following the line of fishing wire, Joe finally saw her.

"Roxanne!", Joe squealed in surprise, not expecting to see her alive.

From the kitchen doorway he could see she was wearing a formal black dress and that she too was tapped to a wooden chair that was tilted backwards on a forty-five-degree angle, leaving her head resting in the kitchen sink which was overflowing with water.

"Don't come any closer Joe!", Roxanne yelled out, as the Toaster came swinging in from the top of the kitchen cupboards like a robotic Tarzan, using its electrical cord to propel itself onto the kitchen counter as it landed directly in the middle of Joe and Roxanne.

"I HOPE YOU ENJOY DINNER. TONIGHT, IT'LL BE BRAINS...A LA BEIGE!", shrieked the Toaster, pulling the fishing wire down with its small metal arms, causing all three heads of the Beige family to pop open simultaneously like a meaty champagne cork. Pieces of bone and brain tissue flew outwards under the pressure, leaving the top of their skulls hanging half a foot above their open craniums like a sadistic tree ornament of horror.

Mrs. Beige and her son had their brains exposed with an assortment of herbs and spices sprinkled on top as they boiled away in their own cerebral broth. Cornelius' cavity was left open and empty with his eyes sunken into the void where his brain once was, staring blankly into Joe's soul.

Coughing up a piece of raw brain which had lodged in his throat, Joe straightened up and glared at the Toaster with all the bravado of a baby chicken on an abattoir conveyor belt, staring down the commercial sized blender, awaiting its nuggety fate with a singular 'cheep-cheep'.

"YOUR BRAIN WILL BE DESSERT!", wailed the Toaster, propelling itself backwards off the kitchen counter and landing on the sink next to Roxanne. It began to stroke her hair with its claws and kept its red eyes fixated on her scalp, drawing blood and causing Roxanne to thrash her head in pain.

"STOP! Leave her be! I'm what you want you little freak, take me instead", Joe begged as he threw the trowel down and extended his arms outwards like the martyr he was.

"That won't be necessary my child", came *The Master's* voice from inside the lounge room, "while my beautiful machine is enthusiastic in its endeavour to retrieve your brain, it's somewhat fixated on preparing it as a meal. That simply will not do...not for you anyway. Stand down my loyal subject, you have done well."

The red eyes of the Toaster turned to amber and its arm's retracted back inside its body, obeying *The Master's* order and remaining stationary by Roxanne's head.

"Now that you know what I am capable of, come sit with me and let's discuss this. You have my word, she will not be harmed", shrilled *The Master*.

Roxanne wept uncontrollably in her restrained position, leaving Joe feeling hopeless and seriously doubting his decision of coming to her rescue.

"I'm sorry", Joe pined and turned his back to Roxanne, her sobs intensified with every step he took away from her, as he made his way to the dimly lit lounge room where *The Master* was waiting.

"Yesssss….yessssss...yesssss...", yearned *The Master* in a creepier manner than that one Great Aunty who demands a kiss on the lips and lets it linger, allowing her recently shaved moustache stubble to tickle the inside of your nostrils.

Stalking *The Master's* chair as he entered the lounge room, Joe caught a glimpse of Brandon's feet hanging off the wall. They were no longer kicking and there was a significant amount of blood running down his leg and pooling onto the wooden floorboards.

"Brandon! Are you alright?!", Joe shouted, but Brandon could only return a lame grunt in response.

"Closer child, closer", commanded *The Master*, stroking something in his lap as all cheap villains have done before him.

"What is that?", Joe queried walking ever so closer.

He could feel the heat of the fire on his face now as

he stood but meters away from the cracked leather seat, staring into the back of *The Master's* incredibly rounded head, covered by a musky smelling hood.

"Oh, this little thing? I'm glad you asked", *The Master* wickedly exclaimed, extending his hand outwards which was holding a pale pink brain dripping in cerebrospinal fluid and blood. *The Master* jiggled it for his own amusement before placing it back on his lap and stroking it tenderly.

"Mr. Beige's brain here is certainly living up to its family name", *The Master* stated, inspecting the brain as its lively pink colour slowly receded away. "He simply...LOST HIS MIND when he heard you were coming for dinner. Ha!"

The Master tilted his head to the side as deafening silence followed, disappointed in Joe's lack of humour at his obtuse pun.

"Enough of the subtleties!", screeched *The Master*, casting the fleshy blob of Mr. Beige's once conscious mind into the fire. It crackled as it landed on a large hollow log, sending black smoke up the fireplace chimney.

Seated as still as an unsuspecting piñata at an armless amputee convention, *The Master* placed his metallic fingers together as if praying to the devil himself. "You will stop playing these silly games now my child and come with me to my lair, or else Roxanne will be…SHOCKINGLY disappointed".

Roxanne screamed from inside the kitchen.

Joe revolved his head on the spot and saw the Toaster's once amber eyes flick back to a blood red. It dipped its pronged arm into the overflowing kitchen sink and electrified Roxanne for five gruelling seconds.

"Ok, ok! I accept", he begged *The Master* desperately.

Joe swung his head back around with confidence, clenched his fists tight with anger, ground his teeth with rage, stared intently with malice, planted his legs with conviction and primed his colon for action.

Joe pushed and strained, his face turning redder than a genetically enhanced tomato giving birth to a punnet of cherry tomatoes. So far Joe's digestive system called the shots sub-consciously, betraying him at the worst of times. This time it was Joe who was in control.

Knowing he couldn't single handily fight his way out of this crappy situation, Joe decided to make a crappy situation of his own.

Neck veins pulsating and blood vessels bursting, Joe

released the most pungent shart to ever grace his homeless man's birthday jocks, and that's no simple feat. The shart spluttered like a dying car engine backfiring, forcing his butt cheeks to slap together louder than a wind-up clapping monkey who has buttocks for hands. The force of the shart blew outwards like stinky ball bearings from a rectal shotgun blast, tearing holes in Joe's underwear and leaving his jeans in a critical condition.

"Sweet Jesus' prostate!", screamed *The Master*, bending his enormous head forward and burying it into his metallic hands as he dry-reached with every breath. The heat from the fire increased the potency of the stench exponentially as the shart evolved into a fully formed biological weapon spreading around the room.

"I'm sorry", lied Joe hiding his grin, "You just make me so nervous. I'm definitely going to need a change of clothes now, unless you want me stinking out your lair."

Holding a palm outward and gesturing Joe to give him a moment, *The Master* leant forward and belched chunks of piping hot vomit on the Persian rug at his feet.

With a new boldness creeping into his once cowardly laced veins, Joe took this opportunity to leverage the situation in his favour.

"Let me take Brandon too. He's bleeding out and needs medical attention. Keep Roxanne as collateral, you know I won't do anything stupid as long as you have her", Joe proposed as loudly as he could, trying to drown out *The Master's* incessant heaving.

"So...young. So...naive", *The Master* snarled, regaining his composure, "I will give you this pardon, but know this. If you're not back before midnight, we will slow cook Roxanne's head like a Sunday roast and serve her to you on a platter...Sally forth young Joe"

Joe didn't wait for the warmth to return to his blood following *The Master's* sadistic monologue. He wasted no time in removing the sharp-edged piece of toast from Brandon's shoulder, waking him from his unconscious slumber with a cry of discomfort as Joe lowered him slowly to his feet.

"No time to talk man, we need to go now. Can you run?", Joe whispered in Brandon's ear.

Brandon shook his head groggily from left to right and gave Joe a half-hearted double thumbs up, "I'm with you dude. Explain this shitfight to me later".

Joe timidly nodded back, not wanting to give *The*

Master any indication of hope which might give away his true intentions.

•

Chapter Eight
Insert Training Montage Here

Joe dragged, carried, pushed and willed Brandon onwards to Bob's caravan. Checking his watch more than the elderly check their incontinence pads, Joe realized they had under three hours to figure out *The Master's* weakness and exploit it before midnight struck.

Bob greeted them at the door to his twenty-foot-long sky-blue caravan which was hidden under dense bushes and camouflaged with green netting. Wearing a black singlet with red shorts and sandals, Bob tried hard to hide his concern behind those reflective aviators and that ridiculous moustache-mullet combination. A far cry from that seductive librarian who stole my heart. You're a cruel harlot Bob.

Brandon wailed as Bob picked him up over his shoulder and carried him up the caravan's side steps. Joe followed behind, locking the heavy steel door with one of the dozen deadlocks installed.

The interior was a paradise that all part time actors dream of when they aren't in a deep alcoholic depression about being actors. Tin mesh lined the walls with an assortment of disguises ranging from clown outfits to ballet tutus. And then there were some more concerning latex variants.

Each had a set of drawers underneath containing all the accessories required for each ensemble. Joe lost count at fifty different sets of disguises when he reached the rear of the caravan. On the left-hand side was a simple single bed, made neatly with only one picture stuck to the ceiling above it.

A picture of Joe when he was eight years old…

Bob laid Brandon down on the bed carefully, propping his injured shoulder up with a pillow to reduce the bleeding.

"Whatever impaled you made a clean cut, the bleeding is only superficial. Here, take these …umm pain killers…yeah that's what they are", said Bob tediously, examining the wound closely, dipping his aviators down and exposing his black but sympathetic eyes. Brandon tilted his head forward accepting the round yellow gelatine pills without question.

Joe felt something was off about Bob having that photo of him above his bed, however, with the countdown to midnight on fast approach he thought better than to ask.

Opposite the bed was a simple kitchen with tall wooden stools lined up at the far end. Joe sat down facing the bed and slumped forward with his head in his hands. Bob's meaty hand clasped down on Joe's shoulder with a gentle squeeze.

"I know you have a lot on your mind boy, but I have to show you something that's seriously important if you're wanting to go back there", Bob straddled the stool next to Joe and looked at Brandon lying peacefully, "Otherwise, if you don't make it back here in time you'll reset at midnight and forget everything."

Joe sighed loudly. The burden of saving Roxanne weighed more on him than the time Aileen tied his manhood to a cinderblock and dangled it out of the top floor window, after finding out Joe tried to smuggle dirty magazines into school. Some call it child abuse. I call it good old-fashioned child abuse!

Much like his overstretched appendage, Joe's mental capacity was at its limit. Weakly smiling at Bob through his hands, Joe nodded, "Go on Bob, we need all the help we can get."

Without warning, Brandon sprung up from the bed, and sat straighter than Joe's mangled one-eyed snake ever could.

"Bob you magnificent man!", Brandon cried out,

pivoting on his rear and flinging his legs over the bed to face Joe whose slack jawed mouth was open wide in awe. Brandon removed the crude bandage Joe had placed over his injury on their way to Bob's caravan and revealed no wound.

Turning his head to the side like a sexually confused tortoise, Joe stared at Bob desperately seeking answers. "What the hell were in those pills Bob?"

"Now boys, it's important to know the science behind the answer before I tell you-", Bob started.

"C'mon Bob! This is amazing! Tell us first", pleaded Brandon, with more energy than a cocaine addicted seahorse, which begs the question. How does a seahorse use cocaine underwater?

"No seriously boys, I need to tell you the backstory first-"

"Bob! Dude! We can defeat *The Master* if we're invincible, what is it?", Joe jumped off his stool, invigorated by this display of seemingly powerful magic.

"I'm not mucking around now boys-"

"BOB! Pleeeeeeeeeeeease. Tell us, tell us, tell us, tell us-", chanted Joe and Brandon, feeding off each other's excitement as they eagerly awaited some mind-blowing reveal.

"ITS URINE ALRIGHT...ITS YOUR URINE BRANDON", Bob yelled, turning the excitable chant into a horrifically awkward silence as Brandon and Joe sat back down slowly, first looking at each other, then at the exit and finally back to each other. "Now before you go all squeamish and freak out, let me explain."

"You sick motherfu-", Brandon stopped himself midway, "Wait! How'd you get my urine?"

"That's your first question? Not how it cured you or why? Jesus Brandon, if I didn't know you any better, I'd be disappointed", hissed Bob, standing up and adjusting his red short-shorts that rode up his crutch higher than a questionable 1970's sports coach.

"I got it from the dead version of you in the warehouse. I siphoned it from his bladder just in case we needed it", Bob turned his back to the boys, opening a large wooden cupboard above the kitchen sink.

"Ahh...sooo Brandon can heal people by pissing on them?", Joe questioned with a hint of sarcasm. Even after all he had endured, this prospect was still too ridiculous to believe.

"Not exactly boy. He can only heal himself, and the specimen has to be taken from outside the time-bubble for it to work", Bob turned back around holding several large jars filled with an assortment of yellow and brown gelatine tablets, pastes and liquids.

"I gave you the same thing Joe when I had you in the Ambulance, but that dose was only meant to return your memories to you"

"Ok let's back this bad boy up a little. Maybe we should have started with that explanation first!", Brandon admitted, holding his stomach as the smell of stale urine and putrefied faecal matter wafted over from the jars Bob had placed on the small kitchen bench.

Hold onto your giblets!

I don't know about you, but I'm not sitting through another mind numbing, soul crushing 'Bob's guide to Doomsville'.

How about a cliché flashback where the background becomes wavy and wind chimes ring out as the picture blurs away instead?

No...well too bad because it's happening.

•

2 YEARS AGO

It had been one year since the time-bubble event had occurred which Bob referred to as the 'Dissolution of Interspace Continuity Kinematics', and what a DICK it was.

Bob spent the year hunting and gathering materials from inside the time-bubble at night, but more often than not Bob returned home with no memory of how or why he got there.

During this time, Bob hypothesised that the DICK strikes at midnight, penetrating your unprotected mind and resetting your days' worth of memories. Pushing his High School Chemistry knowledge to its limit, Bob set out to create a 'Counter Orbital Neurological Dissolution Obstruction Mechanism' to prevent the DICK from causing any further damage.

Working on the basis that the DICK sent out 'Seismic Electromagnetic Microwaves of Energy Neuroinhibitors' causing short term memory loss, Bob tried to make the CONDOM fit for that theory. Unfortunately, no matter what combination of Neuro Blockers he ingested or how strong a magnetic field he tried to surround himself with, the DICK kept on firing its SEMEN at midnight and broke through every CONDOM he made, soaking his mind and erasing the day.

After weeks of having SEMEN splash across his brain, Bob realized that he needed a biological component to complement the current CONDOM he was using.

To overcome the DICK, Bob needed a 'Hippocampus Activator of Neurostabalising Development', and it would need to be a strong HAND indeed to beat the DICK on a daily basis.

Bob started by using samples of his biological fluids mixed in with the current CONDOM he had. Blood had a temporary effect. Sweat had none. Ear wax was completely useless. Mucus was too thick to dissolve. Belly button fluff was too coarse and toe jam too sticky.

Weeks of trial and error led to the unthinkable...Waste products. The theory was based around using all your concentration and thoughts to remember everything about your day's events while you expelled the waste. The energy transfer from your short-term memory in the Hippocampus would cross over into the brains Cortex which controls higher thoughts, as well as the bladder and bowel.

Placing the waste product in a gelatine tablet, Bob coated the outside with an ion exchanged resin mixed with a hydrophilic base, making it a slow release dosage.

With monk like meditation, Bob would strain and struggle to release the perfect brown nugget of memory, and the ideal yellow stream of daily recollection. He called this part of the process, the 'Visceral Autonomous Secretion of Elective Concentration Telepathy into Outward Memory Yielding'.

Armed with his new weapon, Bob set out into Doomsville just prior to midnight, ingesting his freshly prepared tablets. The DICK was no match for Bob's mighty HAND. When midnight struck, no matter how much SEMEN was emitted from the DICK, the combination of both the CONDOM and the VASECTOMY prevented all impregnations of the short-term memory.

And so there you have it. As you can imagine, this was a hard pill to swallow for both Joe and Brandon. But when we return to the story thankfully all that boring explanation part is done, and we can move on.

No need to thank me.

•

"Hurry up man! I need the toilet now", Joe begged, holding onto his specimen jars for dear life.

"Dude, I can't pee!", Brandon whined from inside the cupboard sized toilet.

"Well boy, you're just gonna have to settle for the other type of waste then aren't you", Bob jeered.

"Oh dear god no…"

"Less whining, more concentration Brandon. But leave the memory of me in high heels and stockings out", chuckled Bob as he caught the sight of Joe with his back turned and urinating into a cup.

"Um sorry, I was really busting! Oh yeah, more concentration…", Joe said, falling silent as he willed his daily memories into the cup.

After a few minutes of gag inducing stirring and mixing, the boys made their gelatine tablets and downed a dozen of them with some orange juice that Bob promised would reduce the reflux.

Unfortunately for Brandon, his faecal smelling burps were coming out thick and fast, turning the caravan into a death trap which rivalled even Hitler's gas chambers.

"This better work Bob", Brandon pined, covering his mouth as another putrid burp erupted.

"That's the last of our worries man", Joe stood up pointing to his watch, "We only have two hours to get back there, save Roxanne and defeat that Toaster".

"Why not try and take out *The Master* while you're at it?", questioned Bob, giving Joe the same look a less than enthused Math teacher gives their worst student who refuses to accept that Pi is not a food.

"I have a feeling *The Master* can't do anything on his own. He relies on his creations to do his dirty work. I don't think we need to worry about him", Joe thought out loud, speaking to the ceiling of the caravan as if embarrassed to be using his intuition.

"I couldn't agree with you more boy, I've watched on many occasions when *The Master* has tried to kill or take you. Not since before the time-bubble was up has he tried to do it himself…"

Knowing he said something he wasn't meant to, Bob immediately straightened his back and cleared his throat, pushing his aviators hard against his face. "Before you ask Joe, I'll tell you that story after tonight, I promise. For now, let's focus on the task at hand."

Joe had so many questions racing through his mind as he watched Bob walk to the door and exit the caravan, ushering the boys to follow him with a gesture of his hand.

Brandon looked at Joe with a quizzical expression, "I know what you're thinking dude. But he's right for now. Let's focus", Brandon put his hand in the middle of Joe's back and walked him out the caravan door.

'*The Master* attacked me before the time-bubble was up? Why don't I remember?', Joe pondered.

It was a short walk through the dense bush that led the group to the rear of the abandoned warehouse.

The floor to the warehouse had been cleared of rubble and cleaned. Now, a large metal bench was set up at one end, and over a dozen metal toasters were placed at regular intervals along it. A string of temporary festive fairy lights hung over the bench, illuminating the workspace but leaving the rest of the large warehouse in darkness.

"You've been busy Bob", Joe said coldly.

Even after everything Bob had done for them, Joe couldn't help but feel there was something missing. Bob never came to help them with *The Master*, even though he was the most capable. Could it be that he was in on the plot to capture Joe? Could Bob be *The Master*? Could it be that I'm just feeding you some misdirection?

For now, Joe had no choice but to trust him.

Bob walked out from the shadows wearing a green medical gown, a long white beard and a large prosthetic nose. Bob waved the boys over closer to the bench while rubbing his cleanly shaven head.

Shrugging their shoulders in a sign that they were now so desensitized to Bob's extravagant displays of disguise, the boys meandered over and inspected the plethora of ingredients laid out in front of each toaster.

"In order for you to defeat the Toaster, you must prevent it from using its strongest weapon. Its toast ejector", Bob pointed to Brandon's shoulder, sending phantom pains along his arm and causing him to grab at the old wound site.

"In front of you is every known superglue, adhesive and all-round sticky stuff I could find. I've tried every conceivable combination, but I've been unable to create a substance strong enough to block the toast ejector in under thirty seconds", Bob dropped both hairy hands flat on the bench with a thud that jolted Joe.

"Any idea's boys?"

Joe looked at Brandon. Brandon looked at Joe. Bob looked at Joe and Brandon through the reflection on the bench, showing Joe looking at Brandon who was looking at Bob.

Joe nodded to Bob. Bob nodded to Brandon. Brandon nodded at Joe and Bob while Bob nodded back to Joe and Brandon, leaving Joe nodding to himself.

They all nod at you, the reader.

You nod back to the book, like an idiot.

They had a plan!

•

Chapter Nine

It Comes After Chapter Eight

11:50pm

The Beige's house was in darkness, all except for the flickering light seeping out of the front lounge room. The front door was wide open and as inviting as an opportunity for a double leg amputee to compete in a three-legged sack race.

There was no need for Joe or Brandon to execute their toddler level ninja skills this time. Walking tall and proud, they both entered the house with more testosterone then an Alpha male bull following several rounds of intense chemotherapy.

"Cutting it close my child. I'm afraid that's my job!", *The Master* critiqued from inside the lounge room. "But it appears you've honoured our deal. How predictably pathetic."

Joe rolled his shoulders forward and slumped his head down with Brandon following suit. If they wanted any chance of success, they needed *The Master* to be blinded by his own ego. With a fake bloodied bandage tying Brandon's right arm across his chest and over his shoulder, Brandon committed himself to act like a dying swan. Something that came all too naturally.

"Release Roxanne, you have me now", Joe sulked, keeping up his cowardly appearance.

"Very well my child, it makes no difference to me", *The Master* waved his right metallic hand outwards from his seated position, "she is released...from LIFE!"

Joe spun his head toward the kitchen, unable to see Roxanne's figure at the sink. Only now the chair she was previously tied to was lying on its side, soaked in blood.

Brandon grabbed Joe's hand and squeezed it as hard as he could, whispering in his ear, "Whatever he's done, don't let it get to you dude. We have to stick to our plan. She'll come back."

Joe closed his overcrowded teeth together like a vice, much harder than a priest attempting to convert a goat away from a life of Satanism. Blasphemous goats!

He looked around the room, desperate to see where Roxanne was. *The Master* sensed Joe's frustration, "Ah, you never could see beyond your own nose my child. Or should I say, UNDER YOUR FEET! Mwa ha haaa"

Joe and Brandon froze. With the subtlest of movements Joe felt the rug slide under his shoes. Both their heads lowered down with the speed and suspense you'd expect from a B-grade horror movie.

There she was. Flayed and displayed under their feet like a skinned bear. Joe and Brandon jumped off the meaty human rug screaming like piglets. *The Master* cackled loudly at the sight and clapped his metal hands together, causing a death melody to ring throughout the house.

"It never gets old. But then again…neither do you my child", *The Master* riddled.

Joe's secret weapon against *The Master* was that he didn't realise Joe knew the truth about the time-bubble.

"What the hell do you mean by that?", Joe yelled, playing his part as he shuffled closer to *The Master's* chair, one inch at a time.

"Those questions and more will be answered. Once I have your BRAIN!", *The Master* screeched.

Intune with its creator's voice, the barbaric Toaster abseiled down from the rafters above Joe using a power cord extender and landed in between *The Master* and the boys.

"Kill his friend and tie Joe up", *The Master* ordered, clicking his fingers as he stared ahead into the roaring fireplace.

Coagulated blood oozed off the Toaster's crumb tray mouth as two forked arms extended out from its sides and it fixed its red eyes on Brandon.

"Wait!", Brandon pleaded, "Before you kill me, please let me have one slice of delicious golden toast...for all times sake?"

"What?", *The Master* cried with a strained voice, "Kill him already!"

"Dude, what are you doing? Run already", Joe begged as well as he could.

The Toaster's eyes flickered red to green as its primary function to toast bread overrode its creators' orders. "MUST FULFILL MY PRIMARY FUNCTION..."

"ARGH! Very well. Make toast, then kill him!", demanded *The Master.*

"YES MASTER", the Toaster barked back, scanning its surroundings, "NEED BREAD... CANNOT LOCATE BREAD."

Brandon patted his pants with his free arm and then looked up in fake surprise, "I always carry a spare sandwich in case of emergencies! Oh bugger, it's a cheese sandwich though. You won't be able to toast that…I guess you'll just have to kill me then. What a shame…."

"Brandon you're not making any sense! Go! Save yourself", Joe threw himself on his knees weeping crocodile tears.

Unfortunately for Joe, his knees sunk into the flappy scalp of Roxanne, sticking to his legs like well-fitting gardening pads.

"MUST FULFILL MY PRIMARY FUNCTION. GIVE ME THE SANDWICH. THEN YOU DIE!", bellowed the Toaster, scuttering forward and snatching the sandwich Brandon held out.

"HA! If you fools think for one second that I don't know what game you're playing, then think again! Anything you put in that sandwich will have no effect. I've made the Toaster impervious to all man-made elements!", *The Master* pompously postulated, raising both arms in the air from his seated position.

The Toaster began to shudder. Steam rose from its bread receptors as its red eyes changed to amber. "MASTER…WHAT…IS…HAPPENING…"

"Maybe man made…" Brandon began.

"…But definitely not made from man", finished Joe,

rising to his feet while wiping the fake tears from his face and removing Roxanne's fleshy face mask from his knees.

It took only a matter of minutes earlier that evening at the warehouse for Brandon and Joe to combine the most powerful adhesive known to man.

With a quick trip back to Aileen's house they found the cheddar cheese that had been aging in Joe's Godfather's rancid underwear for the past three years. Once the cheese was pried off the undergarments with a commercially graded spatula, they mixed in a sprinkle of Aileen's toenail gunk which was used to help set the Christmas pudding, infected ear wax from all fifteen cats and the leftovers of Joe's last epic conjunctivitis episode which was so brutal, its contents were locked in a biohazard jar ready to be sent to the State's Centre for Disease for analysis.

"Ha ha haaaa", laughed *The Master* manically, "I've built a failsafe into the Toaster, so if it cannot eject anything it explodes with the force of a one megaton bomb! I'm ready to die...are you?"

Joe looked at Brandon with a horrified expression. This wasn't part of their plan but somehow Brandon looked as calm as ever. Joe immediately knew what he was thinking. Brandon walked over to the malfunctioning Toaster, picked it up with both arms and in a bear hug, pressed the ejector ports to his chest.

Without speaking the words, Brandon mouthed 'I'll see you again' to Joe.

"My mother was a hen?"

'I'll see you again'

"You loved a man named Ben?"

'I. Will. See. You. Again' Brandon mouthed even slower.

"Ahhh", Joe sighed, "So what if you wanna be known as Jen? I'm cool with that dude!"

Brandon rolled his eyes and clasped his hands around the Toaster, pulling it towards him. The sound was deafening.

The crunch of Brandon's chest cavity as it caved inwards. The snapping of his ribs as they were splayed outwards, tearing through his torso. The bloody rattle of Brandon's last breath through his shredded lungs. The crumpling of his lifeless body falling to the floor and the subsequent slushing of his intestines flowing onto the custom-made Roxanne rug.

"Sweet Grandmothers Clitoris!", *The Master* rose

from his chair and lifted his hood back over his engorged cranium as he pulled a release lever near the fireplace, cutting the oxygen to the fire. The room fell into darkness with only the ominous glow of the full moon cutting through the overdramatic setting.

Joe stood still, unsure what to do. He knew Brandon's sacrifice would not be in vain. He knew that in just under five minutes both Brandon and Roxanne would be reanimated in their beds, alive and safe with no knowledge of their horrible demise. But why did he still feel such guilt and despair?

Turning to face Joe in the shadows, *The Master* stepped forward to inspect his melted invention covered in unbreakable strands of super stringy smelly cheese. Speaking with only the mildest of disappointment in his tone, "Tssk Tssk. Not even salvageable"

"Go on! You have me now you bastard. Why won't you be a man and fight!", Joe was only a few meters away but still *The Master's* face eluded him.

"Ah I wouldn't be so prudent my child, I tried that once…", as *The Master* spoke, he lifted up his metal hands, "Let's just say, our chemistry on contact is volatile to say the least. No, no. Patience is my virtue. When you've lived as long as I have…well let's not get into that."

As *The Master* walked to the front door to leave, Joe stepped between him and the exit. He wanted nothing more than to kill this anti-Christ of Mormon proportions, but some unknown force was clouding his mind the closer he got to *The Master*. It was as if they were two magnets of a similar charge being forced together, only to be repelled back again.

"Fear not my child. I will return", *The Master* pushed a metal hand outward towards Joe's face stopping only inches from him. The pain and confusion were excruciating, forcing Joe to take a step back.

"Ha! I enjoy our little moments together. I will miss our battles when you're gone", *The Master* approached the front door as Joe regained his composure.

"I know who you are!"

It all made sense to Joe now. He'd been lured into a false trust by an excellent manipulator who was conveniently never there when the actual Master was. It left only one answer.

The Master stopped in his tracks, one foot hovering out the doorway. Without turning around, he spoke with a slight curiosity as his voice raised up an octave, "I'm listening"

"Bob! You son of a bitch, you're Bob!", Joe was feeling his energy return to him the further he was from *The Master*. He put it down to the tablets Bob gave him. 'He had this planned all along, get me to take the tablets to make me weak when I faced him'.

The Master fell to his knees. Choking.

Wait he wasn't choking. He was laughing.

Soft at first then diabolically loud, slapping his metal hands on the ground and howling at the moon in fits of explosive cackles.

"Admit it! I'm not falling for any more of your traps Bob", Joe leant over Brandon's mangled corpse and pulled a fire poker from the fireplace, still red hot at the tip.

Grabbing the sides of the doorway *The Master* heaved himself to his feet, dusting off his long black robe.

"Oh my child, you truly are a treasure. Let me guess, Bob's about this tall...", still facing away from Joe, *The Master* indicated a height with his outstretched right arm, "Hairy hands, red scar under his left eye and is a self-proclaimed master of disguises?"

Joe wasn't sure where *The Master* was going with this, but he was standing by his decision. "Yeah whatever Bob, I'm sick of listening to your bullshit. If anyone could pretend to be *The Master* it'd be you."

Clasping his hands together, *The Master* maneuvered his grotesquely enormous head to looked up at the moon. "Bob, Bob, Bob. How that name has haunted me."

"So you DO admit it!", Joe edged closer with the fire poker raised, feeling the ripples of nausea increase with each step.

The Master lowered his head and spoke softly, "No young one. But seeing as he's your father, perhaps he can tell you who I am...that's if you can even remember to ask! Ha ha ha", with *The Master's* final words, Joe looked down at his watch as it struck midnight.

A large pulse of energy overcame Joe, sending him flying backwards into the chair at the centre of the lounge room. Fog threatened to overcome Joe's consciousness as he searched for any sign of *The Master*, who had since departed.

Bob raced inside a moment later wearing a Santa outfit with extra stomach padding, rushing to Joe and clicking his fingers inches away from his face, "Joe are you alright? Do you remember me?"

Joe winced in pain as he lifted his head and processed his thoughts. 'That pulse must have been the resetting of the time bubble...Wait, I remember the time bubble! And I remember...'

"Yeah I do remember. I remember you...Dad"

•

Carving through the carcass of Brandon's cold corpse, the Cheese Sandwich created from the Toaster's criminal consciousness, carefully crawled closer to the cavities exit, carnivorously craving the cranium and its spoils. Chaotically chomping into the cerebellum with criminal callousness, the Cheesy creation called out for its Creator of Carnage, its Champion of Chaos, its Count of Condolences.

PART III
THE CHEESE SANDWICH OF CARNAGE

Chapter Ten

Of Mice and Men and Brains

In all honesty I never thought I would see you again, figuratively speaking of course. If I could see you then I'd be scarred for life watching you pick your nose constantly while you turn my pages with your unwashed hands on the toilet…don't you dare deny it! Perhaps you have a brain tumour rendering you incapable of making the right decisions, or maybe you were born at the top of the Great pyramid of Giza and landed on your head the whole way down. I'm not here to judge but do yourself a favour and check in for a lobotomy after you finish this book. You're going to need it.

It's been an emotional rollercoaster full of bodily fluids, organs and amputated body parts. My favourite kind.

Not only did we find out that *The Master* created a time-bubble around Doomsville three years ago and has been manipulating every prominent change that has happened in the town since then, but also some weird alien meteorite might be the source of all his power. Who says it's never aliens?

And let's not forget how much of a sexy beast Bob is in those heels!

But surely there needs to be some kind of disclaimer to stop people from trying to cure Alzheimer's by eating memory poo, or urinating on Emergency Department patients to heal their wounds. Get in early with your lawsuit's readers, the writer is broke and vulnerable.

Better yet, someone should really report this misogynistic bastard for giving Aileen and Roxanne the worst possible character arcs and death scenes. Shame on you Mr Steele! No wonder your first name shortens to Dick.

And last but certainly not least, the most overdone twist of all time…Bob is Joe's father who was meant to have died in a cliché and unimportant way!

Now that I have recapped the last Act with more subtlety than a drunk Jehovah's witness making sweet, sweet love to your doorbell, prepare yourself for a gruelling marathon length explanation into the backstory of *The Master*.

It will make the previous explanations in this book look like two of Bob's explanations that got together and had a baby explanation, which is all grown up now and went to Explanation University, got a degree in explaining things and currently works a 9-

5 job at 'Explanation R'Us'. Self explanatory really.

So, strap yourselves in for a tedious and overcomplicated twenty-page enema of truth...

Just kidding! I wouldn't do that to you. After all, reading this much of the book must be harder than reading a cook book for the blind. Unless they have brail. Then it'd be harder than trying to read a cook book for the blind AND handless. Not my best metaphor, but you get my drift.

Alright, so to explain this is a fun and frivolous way, there are three doors with three different pieces of information about *The Master* and his backstory.

One of the doors contains true facts. The other two are false. Let's see how well you think you know this book.

•

DOOR NUMBER 1

I. Majority of humans have already transcended the physical realm and entered themselves into a digital databank. Doomsville is actually no larger than the width of a single cell and Joe is the primary program inside, which is being played by a sadistic twelve-year-old brat on a baron Mars outpost.

II.   *The Master* is a corrupt file within this program, Brandon, Bob, Aileen and Roxanne acting as Joe's personal anti-virus defence system. Sound like a movie you know? It probably is.

III.   Bored with playing this glitch ridden game that resets every twenty-four hours due to it being over a thousand years old, the demonic Martian child decides to play God and inject the Doomsville program into the sperm of a frog and fertilizes it inside the egg of an ostrich. Seen that movie? Didn't think so smarty pants.

IV.   A 'Frogrich' is born and it's as ugly as it sounds. Is it the head of a frog with the legs of an ostrich? Or is it the head of an ostrich with the legs of a frog? Take some time to wrap your head around that...

V.   ...but don't take too much time, because this Frogrich has the consciousness of Joe AND the evil mind of *The Master*. They've both found out the truth behind their existence in the program and have teamed up to seek revenge on this twelve-year-old spawn of Satan.

VI.   Wearing a pair of dark sunglasses, a black leather jacket and a bad attitude, this Frogrich is about to hop into vengeance...or is it running into vengeance? I can't really tell. To be honest, it looks more like a genetically mutated blob on the floor, begging to be put out of its misery.

DOOR NUMBER 2

I.   Joe is not Joe at all. He is being held involuntarily in a chemically induced coma, hidden in an underground human experimentation laboratory run by Buddhist extremists. The experiments involve the splicing of chicken brains into humans, hoping to tap into the unbridled genetic potential of the chicken's distant dinosaur ancestors, and unleash unholy poultry war on the world.

II.   Brandon, Bob, and Aileen are all different parts of Joe's fragmented personality, struggling against the invading spliced chicken brain i.e. *The Master*, who is relentlessly trying to take full control of Joe's brain once and for all. Guess that explains why we don't see many people walking the streets of Doomsville? It wouldn't just be poor writing surely?

III.   The day is set on a loop in Joe's mind because the doctor's dose him every twenty- four hours to keep him in a comatose state. Unbeknown to the underground organization, there is an intelligent race of super advanced chickens from the future who have been monitoring this abomination and are currently fighting the Buddhist extremists in the tenth dimension.

IV.   What about Roxanne you ask? Before Joe was kidnapped, he was a loyal farm-hand on a family owned chicken estate located just outside Doomsville. Joe refused to kill the chickens against his father's orders, sparking a keen interest from the super advanced chicken race from the planet B'ah Kirk. They then sent an ambassador, Princess Ten Der Breasts, to act as a diplomat to Earth, in the hopes of forming a planetary alliance.

V.   Princess Ten Der Breasts and Joe had one summer of forbidden love at Joe's family holiday home near the beach. But before she could tell Joe about their happy chick-child news he was taken away, betrayed by his father who found out about their clucky love. So, sneaking into Joe's mind through advanced telepathy powers, Princess Ten Der Breasts took on the form of Roxanne in his mind to be closer to her one true love.

DOOR NUMBER 3

I.   Doomite is actually a billion year old time travelling entity called… wait for it…'The Entity'. It comes from an ancient part of the universe that predates the Big Bang, seeking out a host in the form of a conscious lifeform so it can feed off free will and enslave blah blah blah sound lazy and unimaginative? That's because it is.

II.   The Entity crashed on Earth just outside Doomsville where it was stored in a warehouse. After several strange deaths involving hammers, chisels and the occasional toothpick coming to life, the local government thought it best to bury the alien rock in the abandoned mines under the town. Ignorance is bliss.

III.   In the not so far future, Doomsville is a town in steep decline, suffering a slow financial death due to numerous highway bypasses and a lack of interest from the country's government for tourism and infostructure. A mass exodus of citizens left *The Master* heartbroken when his closest family and friends left for greener pastures. *The Master* was inconsolable.

IV.   In desperation, *The Master* agreed to bind with The Entity to save a dying Doomsville, only wanting to protect and preserve it to bring his loved ones back to him. Little did *The Master* know that The Entity had no intention of releasing him from this agreement and had greater ambitions then the enslavement of a meagre town like Doomsville.

V.   *The Master* travelled back to specific dates in

Doomsville's history, making changes he thought were in the best interest for the town's future, rewriting the timeline and growing more obsessive with each time jump. The Entity slowly corrupted his ever-growing phallus of a head, filling it with thoughts of world domination until one fateful night he broke a paradoxical law and tried to kill his younger self. Causing a catastrophic tear in the fabric of time, *The Master* was forced to create a time-bubble to protect space-time from collapsing in on itself, consequently trapping himself in an alternative timeline with his younger version. The only thing standing in *The Master's* way of total time travel domination, is the living brain of his counterpart.

•

Phew. Those are some really tough decisions.

If you picked Door number 1 – I have nothing more to say. Seek urgent help!

If you picked Door number 2 – You are reader after my own heart. But alas, it was never meant to be.

If you picked Door number 3 – You officially are the most boring party pooper I've ever met, but you are correct.

Now if that's the case, and correct me if I'm wrong,

but it says *The Master* tried to kill his younger self.

Hmmm. And then it said he needs the brain of his counterpart. Double hmm.

That can only mean...

"Yessss", hissed *The Master*, rudely interrupting my slow and incredibly painful build-up.

Oh shit! It can't be true.

"Oh, but it can and it is, my floating headed friend", mocked *The Master*.

No! Anything but that! Surely we can make it Door number 1. Let's get you a motorbike, a shotgun, a nice lily pad for your Frogrich babies and go mow this twelve-year-old down like good sensible people.

Or maybe Door number 2. Yes, that works for me. It's an eggcellent love story. Don't be such a cluck head Master!

"I'm afraid not", snapped *The Master*, wagging his finger so hard that it waggled with so much wag, he couldn't tell its wiggle from its wobble.

"Enough! I don't have time for this", *The Master* sprayed, checking his retro Casio watch, with built in calculator might I add...

Great Step Mothers diaphragm! It is true.

At the very least the readers deserve to know why

you did it…*Master Joe* from the future.

"Bravo, you are a quick learner", leaning back in his imaginative seat and stroking his imaginative beard, *Master Joe* prepared himself to clear up any loopholes you were just thinking about.

Enter the villains' monologue.

"Let's see, I was fifteen years old when my wretched family and traitorous friends left me and my beloved town. Nothing I said or did kept them from leaving. I dropped out of school so I could work and pay board, but I couldn't afford to keep the family home. I watched as an army of raccoons treated my childhood memories like a rabies playground"

"Everyone thought I was a fool to stay back and fight for this towns survival. Everyone but my sweet Entity."

"Every change I made in the past; the bans, the curfews, the automatic wedgie pickers, they all helped preserve this town…my town. Once I completed my task all I wanted to do was travel back to that moment my parents were wanting to leave. To tell them what I did to save Doomsville and see how proud they were of me"

Melodramatically raising the back of his hand against his forehead and falling to his knees, *Master*

Joe attempts to pluck on your heart strings in an effort to make the villain more relatable. Nice try, we aren't falling for that one.

"One look at how time travel had ravaged my face and my mother broke into tears, refusing to look at me. My father begged me to travel back and undo everything I had accomplished. He told me I was messing with powers I couldn't comprehend. They didn't see that I did this all for them. One nice word was all I needed. One gentle embrace"

Ok, so I'm slowly relating now.

"I held my mother's face in my hands and told her how much I loved her…"

Oh wow, maybe we were wrong about this guy.

"…I looked over to my father and told him how sorry I was…"

Let this be a lesson to all of you about judging a book by its cover…Unless it's this book… In that case definitely judge away because this cover is awesome.

"…I snapped her head clean off her judgemental neck and used it to beat my father unconscious. They weren't going to ruin everything I had done."

Ah there it is! He's back everyone.

"I knew little about the complexities of time travel back then and thought I needed to end the younger version of myself to rid this timeline of any corruption. I crept to my old bedroom and placed my hands around younger Joe's neck. That was the last time I made that mistake. Boom!"

Yeah yeah metal hands, we all get it now.

"I raced back to my sweet Entity with stumps for hands, pleading for its help. It told me what I needed to do. By placing my hands on my younger self, I tore the fabric of time and space, threatening to engulf the world in a miniature black hole if it wasn't properly patched."

Hmm nope, not even my year ten physics education is buying that one but go on.

"In order to fix the rift, I needed to cast a time-bubble over the town until I could safely retrieve the living brain of my younger self. It took three days for me to regain my strength in order to summon that kind of power through The Entity. And the rest...is HISTORY! Get it? He he he."

Jeez, this guy is crazier than a coconut cannibalizing another coconut, while drinking coconut milk from its cracked coconut skull and sunbathing in coconut oil from its coconut heart.

One last question Mr. Coconut. Why Joe's living brain? Other than the fact that it's in the title of this book and we need to drag the story out another two chapters.

"Oh, I have killed Joe. Many, many times. As satisfying as it was to bathe in his blood, it never closed the rift. On further experimentation with countless other…volunteers, The Entity and I concluded that the brain of Joe must be conscious and preserved. I must keep it with me at all times, so it can act like a space-time band-aid of sorts between the two realities. Then I'll be free to take over THE WORLD! HAHA"

Clap.

Clap.

Clap.

There you have it folks. The moment you have all been waiting for and wasted multiple hours of your short dull lives getting to, only to find out it was about as satisfying as a leper giving out free hugs.

Might as well see how it ends now. Unless you're the type of person who throws out toilet rolls when they still have one or two sheets left. Yes you. You know who you are…

•

Chapter Eleven
Who's Your Daddy

Six peaceful months have passed since we last saw our loveable friends. Shortly after the reset at Roxanne's house, Joe and Bob snuck over to Brandon's house while the reanimated version of him slept, recalibrating his memories with the pills they had made the previous day. Then Aileen was brought into the fold, although Joe had his suspicions she knew the truth all along.

Joe was hesitant about including Roxanne into their group and thought it was safest for her if he left her alone. This didn't stop Roxanne from calling every day to ask him about organising their date. He had rejected her past 181 calls over the last six months, now it was slowly eating away at his soul whenever he heard the disappointment in her voice time and time again.

As a group, they devised a strategy to sneak out of Doomsville each night to Bob's caravan and resupply their ...memory stockpiles. Bob would change his disguises daily and join Aileen, Joe and Brandon for breakfast. Brandon called his parents every morning to tell them he stayed over at Joe's house, and like clockwork their reset minds agreed and thought nothing of it.

Joe felt a deep sense of guilt that his best friend was staying at his house and away from his family for so long. Brandon was always in high spirits though, reminding Joe that it kept his family safe and that they needed to stick together.

Bob and Joe moved past their initial father-son difficulties after Bob explained exactly why he disappeared the way he did on the night his mother died. In painful detail Bob recounted the memory of how another, older version of Joe came to their house that night and the horrors they faced. Joe forgave him almost immediately, knowing full well the pain his father must have endured and being so close but so far away from his son for the past three years.

Armed with the knowledge that *The Master* was Joe from the future, the group formulated a strategy of their own to end this hellish nightmare and rid themselves of this life of days on repeat. All except Aileen, who relished at the idea of living forever and never aging, constantly poking at the inflamed pustules that riddled her face and gloating that she will never again be this beautiful.

The plan was simple. Locate the source of *Master Joe*'s power and destroy it.

Months of reconnaissance, deductive reasoning and over the top hints by yours truly, led the group to believe that the abandoned mines were located under Doomsville Central Park, which was at the epicentre of the time-bubble. The only problem was the silence.

A silence so deafening that if a Mime blew into a foghorn in the cold vacuum of space, recorded that silence and then played it back on the lowest possible volume, it would sound like a rock concert compared to this kind of silence.

Master Joe and his creations were nowhere to be found and the team knew this was not good news. Good news was when Aileen decided to stop using cat litter in the oatmeal and use old shredded baby diapers instead. They couldn't strike at the heart of *Master Joe*'s lair until he popped his big head up like a perverted whack-a-mole game.

After watching his son return the brick sized phone back onto its receiver following another Roxanne rejection, Bob put a hand under Joe's drooping chin, lifting it up and staring sympathetically into his eyes.

"Son, if we let this bastard affect our lives like this

then he might as well take your brain right here and now. Call her back and go on your date, just this one time. She mightn't remember you bailing on her every day, but you do. I can see it eating you up inside", his smile always comforted Joe, especially when it was his real teeth and not a set of his fake vampire teeth.

"I can't take that kind of risk dad", Joe slouched down into the small mice infested lounge which was holier than a piece of Swiss cheese blessed by the Pope, who went on to be crucified by the Tasty Cheese Church for failing to follow the Cheddar way. That's no Gouda.

"I'll be watching like I always have son. Go get ready", Bob stated proudly, ruffling up Joe's dandruff-ridden hair, snowing down on the coffee table made of Aileen's disused tampon boxes, turning it into a menstrual winter wonderland.

Smiling wide and dripping with more confidence than a freshly glazed donut competing in a 'World's Sexiest Baked Goods' competition, Joe picked up the phone and forgot his troubles.

•

Wearing his dead Godfathers two-sizes-too-big green tuxedo and slicking his hair back with so much grease, he looked as though he should have a restraining order preventing him from approaching small school children. Joe was ready for a hot date.

"Oh Joey my boy, you're gonna break hearts", cooed Aileen as she grabbed Joe's cheeks with her crab-like claw hands, pulling them apart and releasing them with enough kinetic energy to launch a rocket into the stratosphere. Oh, but not the cheeks on his face, no…His butt cheeks.

Pulling out a wedgie that threatened to invade his oesophagus, Joe strutted out of the house with more sass than Captain Sassypants the Sasquatch, who lead the sassiest army of sassy Sasquatches in the Great War on Sass.

With woops and cheers from Bob and Brandon, and Aileen throwing a strange grey confetti from an earn that had his late Godfathers name engraved on it, Joe made his way out to the street as a new man, emboldened by this freedom and looking forward to seeing his sweet, innocent, still not really his girlfriend because he lacks the commitment to ask her and she will surely find someone else, Roxanne.

Quickly rounding the corner for their 5pm rendezvous at the only restaurant in Doomsville, 'Doom-Appétit' located just opposite the Library, Joe entered the scantly lit coffin shaped building ten minutes early hoping to have time to cool his nerves and make a good impression.

'Oh shit, does my breath smell that bad?!', Joe thought to himself as a wall of thick musk hit him in the face. Checking his breathed on his hand, Joe smelt the pine scented toilet disinfectant Aileen gave him for good luck. 'Nope, not me.'

Looking around at the dimly lit and completely empty room would have made the Joe from six months ago turn and run for his life. But unfortunately for Joe, that time of peace had made him soft and dumb. Unbelievably dumb. Incomprehensibly stupid, incredibly unintelligent, staggeringly brainless, outlandishly imbecilic and many other various synonyms with adjectives that are so moronic they couldn't even find their way onto this paragraph to help me berate Joe further.

A table reservation sign written in red ink seeping down the place card spelt out 'Joe and Roxy' and was sitting on a table for two in the furthest corner of this small but cosy restaurant. The sides of the room were covered in an outdated red velvet wallpaper, offsetting a dark brown carpet which would make even the most hardcore LSD junkie cringe. The lighting was so poor that when Joe sat down, he could barely see his hands in front of his face.

'Roxy?', he thought to himself as the gears in his chestnut sized brain sluggishly turned, reminding him of all the other times Roxanne was referred to as Roxy, leading him ever so lethargically to the conclusion that...

"Joe?", came Roxanne's voice from across the table, her olive-skinned hand crossing the void between them and landing on top of Joe's hand, sending shivers of teenage hormones up his spine and clouding his judgement.

"Oh Roxanne, I'm so happy you're here. I didn't hear you come in", sighed Joe, leaning back into his chair, feeling secure and relieved.

"Sorry my chi...I mean Joe. I've been waiting here patiently for you, my prince, to arrive. I even booked the whole restaurant for us, just in case you were wondering why it's only us here and no chef, waiter, receptionist or other witnesses...I mean customers", said sweet, innocent and definitely not anyone else pretending to be her in any kind of elaborate trap, Roxanne.

"Wow, you did all this for me?", chuffed Joe, diverting all remaining brain power to the peanut sized appendage between his legs, rather than the obvious threat.

"I can't wait any longer lover boy, give me a kiss",

Roxanne demanded, leaning over so Joe could just see the outline of her mouth, with her thick red lips coming out from the darkness.

'Sweet Eskimos nipples! It's really gonna to happen!', Joe reaffirmed himself as he leant forward and closed his eyes, puckering his lips with as much puck as a puckered blowfish.

And just like putting a baby in a blender thinking it will clean it, he was wrong. So wrong, that if being right was wrong, I'd be a banana and you'd be the split. If you can't see how wrong that is, then maybe you're right...

Her lips felt ice cold as Joe stuck his tongue in and around Roxanne's open and unmoving mouth, causing Joe to draw back from the lingering kiss.

"Is everything alright?", he asked, wiping what appeared to be red lipstick from his lips, leaving a metallic taste in his mouth.

"Yes of course my love", said Roxanne as her face retreated to the shadows once more, "You just gave me the kiss of...DEATH!"

Blinding lights turned on in every corner of the room as a maniacal laugh filled the restaurant, causing Joe to clench his rectum harder than a gorilla strangling a cold hotdog for being an oxymoron. Pushing himself up from his seat while shielding his burnt retina's, Joe's vision finally cleared and unveiled a sight that not even Medusa could look at.

There she was. Roxanne. Sweet, innocent, now strung up like a human puppet and never going to be Joe's girlfriend because he can't rescue a turd from a toilet bowl, Roxanne.

Stringy yellow strands were screwed into Roxanne's scalp, lips, upper arms, lower legs, hands and feet. Dried blood stained the skin where the strands were inserted as they poked out the other side of each limb like a needle and thread. Roxanne's bulging dead blue eyes stared into nothingness as the strands were pulled upwards, forcing her lifeless body to dance to an old jazz tune. Her bones and cartilage crackled and protruded outwards through her skin, ripping holes in her yellow floral dress as the puppet master above her fought through the onset of rigor mortis.

"What's the matter my child?", *Master Joe* cried out in joy, emerging from the double doored kitchen behind Joe, clapping his hands in delight. The Roxanne-puppet jumped on the table and kicked her legs out as if dancing the Can Can, her mouth moving up and down as *Master Joe* crudely imitated her voice, "Ohhh lover boy, come give me another kiss."

Joe thought he'd seen everything after sailing his metaphorical ship of synonyms on *Master Joe*'s sadistic sea of sadism, but no amount of nonsensical alliteration could comfort him. His arms and legs shook violently with pure unadulterated hatred for his future self.

"Stop calling me child you sick fu-fudge face", sprayed Joe, forcing the narrator to yet again save the day from these potty mouthed heathens.

"Ahh but that's all you are, just a child", touted *Master Joe*, concealed under his long black hooded robe. His hands were clasped behind his back now as he slowly circled Joe and the table where the Roxanne-puppet was now breakdancing on top of, sending shards of bone and flesh flying as her body fell apart piece by piece while her eyeballs popped out of their sockets, dangling against her once blushed cheeks.

"If there was any shred of me left in you, you'd never do this to Roxanne!" yelled Joe, shying away from the sight of Roxanne's ribs bursting through her abdomen as she spun 360 degrees on her head, sending her kidneys out like miniature ball and chains, crashing onto the nearest table.

"Jealous, are we? My my, Roxanne and I got up to so much more than just a little kiss", *Master Joe* boasted as he stopped at the table and grabbed the back of Roxanne's tenderized head.

Joe's jaw dropped as he looked at Roxanne, then back at *Master Joe* in the same way a horrified mother looks at her son after finding out why he stole her weekly feminine magazine, a pair of her fishnet stockings and a year supply of moisturizer.

"Great Pelican's urethra! No child, I didn't mean here and now! She's only fifteen years old! I meant Roxanne and I got together in the future. That is of course, before she left me like everyone else. Don't make this book any harder to publish then it already is with your immature vulgarity!" spouted *Master Joe*, almost certainly causing Joe to have an existential crisis with the knowledge that he is only a fictional character in a subpar novel.

Fortunately for us, Joe was too distracted by *Master Joe*'s puppet master who was crawling down from the ceiling on its cheesy web of death.

Landing on Roxanne's mutilated body sprawled out on the table, the Cheese Sandwich cut away the remaining cheesy strings that were used to turn her into a dancing zombie.

It was unmistakably the same Cheese Sandwich

they had used to destroy the Toaster of Terror.

Cooked to golden brown perfection, the Cheese Sandwich had two little cheese stick arms and legs, with beady red eyes it inherited from its Toaster predecessor. The indestructible cheesy concoction that Joe and Brandon invented kept both pieces of the bread locked in place, only moving apart like cheddar curtains when it spoke its Feta full of lies.

"Sooo pleased to meet you, young Joe. I must thank you for freeing me from my prison", squealed the Cheese Sandwich as it poked at Roxanne's dried out tongue with a bread stick, sounding more like a gerbil high on helium rather than a cold and calculated lactose intolerants nightmare.

"Who are you?" asked Joe taking a step back, sensing this creation was very different from the mindless robotic demons he'd faced before.

"Joe meet my sweet Entity...Entity meet my younger weaker self", *Master Joe* sat opposite Joe with his gigantic watermelon noggin bowed down, still not ready to reveal his disfigured face to his younger self.

"Entity? You mean the Doomite alien rock which landed here...yeah figured as much. We didn't free you. We killed the Toaster that's all!", Joe spoke with as much bravado as he could muster, eyeing the emergency exit near the kitchen doors and angling his body away from the ever-advancing Cheese Sandwich.

"Ahh good, what you didn't realise was that releasing me into a biological form is something that has alluded *Master Joe* and I for decades. Keeping my power contained in man-made structures reduced my power and influence. Now that I am finally in this form I can replicate at an exponential rate. Soon I will transfer into human bodies and infect the world! Accident or not, I thank you", the Cheese Sandwich said, placing both its hands into its centre where it began to pull itself apart in a mitosis of mayhem, much like watching a jellyfish give birth to a fish made of jelly who begs you to release it from its suffering with a rusty teaspoon.

Joe took this opportunity to take a few more steps back while this re-birth of sticky proportions took place.

"This can't be what you wanted *Master Joe*. It can't be what we wanted", stalled Joe, having no intention of trying to convert *Master Joe* after all the dread he had brought to his life.

'I need to get home and warn the others' Joe willed himself.

Without lifting his beach balled noodle, *Master Joe*

read Joe's mind, "There is no salvation for me here. I waited here at this restaurant for you every day for the past 181 days, torturing and killing Roxanne in new and exciting ways while you left her here all alone. Tell me my child, do you think I'm worth saving now? Go on, tell me how bad The Entity is and that together we can defeat it! Try something corny and stereotypical, I dare you!"

The Cheese Sandwich re-emerged from its melted mix as two individual sandwiches, identical in every way.

"Ha! Oh, I do prefer future Joe to this plain and boring past Joe", one Cheese Sandwich started.

"Yes, he is a well-trained pet. Now, let's get that brain of yours so we can leave this damned town", finished the second sandwich, both jumping to the floor and stalking Joe as if he were a giant pickle.

Joe turned and ran like a gazelle escaping a Gay Pride Parade for drag queen lions, with the devilled deli food gaining on him. Joe knew he was no match for their unbreakable cheesy grip.

'I will not be turned into some reverse Pinocchio for their amusement!', Joe urged to himself on in desperation.

"Say hello to father for me...", yelled *Master Joe* as

Joe burst through the emergency exit with the two sandwiches in hot pursuit.

Tripping over the kitchen bins laid out in the alleyway, Joe landed on his back with both sandwiches jumping on his chest, slowly crawling up to his face and now only inches away.

"Now just hold still…" started the first sandwich, "…it's just like opening an oyster', continued the second sandwich.

They placed their cheese stick hands on either side of Joe's head and started pulling in opposite directions. Joe thrashed and rolled around on the ground, but their grip was too strong they dug their hands deeper into his skull, playing tug of war with his cranium.

There was nothing Joe could do. No one he could call out to for help.

He attempted to break their hold, but it was futile. Their little arms were tougher than a gargoyle's genital warts. Joe could feel his consciousness slipping away as the Cheese Sandwiches' shot cheese cables onto either side of the alleyway walls, pulling themselves in opposite directions and using the walls to winch Joe's head in half.

Peck.

Peck.

"Nooooo!", came a cry from the sandwiches in unison.

Peck.

Peck.

Coo roo-c'oo-coo

'Coo coo..what?', Joe woke from his daze as the pressure on his temples subsided.

Joe sat up faster than a gingerbread man's privates after taking some self-raising flour to help with his impotence. He could feel what was left of the Cheese Sandwiches arms stuck to his hair, swinging in the breeze, but no sign of the sandwiches' themselves.

Dusting himself off and staggering out of the alleyway, Joe saw a flock of head bobbing pigeons decimating the Cheese Sandwiches. I mean, the technical definition of decimation is the removal of a tenth of something, so in this case they were halfinating the Cheese Sandwiches. All the bread was now pecked clean off, leaving only the innards of the once mighty Cheese Sandwiches scattered to the gutters.

'That was a bit of an anti-climax! So much for the ultimate villain', Joe foolishly thought to himself as he wandered home.

Being a sucker for punishment, those thoughts were squashed within minutes as Joe saw fire on the horizon coming from the direction of home.

'I wasn't the target for today…I was the decoy', Joe realized as he ran up his street to find the aftermath of a suburban warzone.

Bread, blood, cheese and organs littered the street with cars overturned and set on fire. Closer to Aileen's house he found Brandon, mummified in a cheesy cocoon and impaled on a streetlight that had plunged through his rectum and out of his mouth. Yes, you guessed it. Another Brendon kebab.

Aileen's amputated hand was still grasping the front door handle as Joe pushed it open and found her body drawn and quartered on the kitchen bench.

"Dad?" Joe yelled, wading through a dozen Cheese Sandwich corpses, some riddled with butter knives, forks and skewers. Many others were torn apart by Aileen's army of cats who were now sitting on their pile of defeated foes with pride.

Covered in blood and condiments, Bob sat on the bottom step of the stairs with a sharpened broom handle in one hand and a waffle pan in the other. Five or so Cheese Sandwiches were skewered onto the broom handle already, while the waffle pan had just finished incinerating two more.

"I'm so sorry dad", Joe began as he sat down next to Bob whose French maid outfit was falling apart. Dropping the broom and waffle pan, Bob leapt at Joe tackling him to the ground.

"What the hell-", Joe yelled in surprised as he slid along the mayonnaise-soaked floor, or in this case, the blood of the vanquished sandwiches.

Bob raised his hands above his head as he stood over Joe, slamming them down over his shoulders and grabbing a Cheese Sandwich that had been crawling up Joe's back with a steak knife in its small cheesy hands.

Using all his brute strength, Bob screamed out loud as he tore the sandwich in half like a primitive ape tearing apart a banana.

Joe was as curious as cat playing Clue who found out that the main character was curiously killed by curiosity itself.

"How'd you manage to do that?", asked Joe as Bob helped him to his feet.

"The more they duplicate, the weaker their cheese bond is", Bob stated exhaustively, falling onto the lounge as his legs gave way.

"Are you hurt?", Joe knelt down next to Bob, stepping in Aileen's bladder and spraying the remaining contents back up into his face.

"No, this isn't my blood...or mayonnaise. Let's get back to my caravan quickly, we can't afford to forget this day or what happened...", Bob trailed off as he closed his eyes, weary from battle.

Wiping his urine-soaked face and regaining his composure, Joe placed his tuxedo jacket over Bob and walked to the front door. "Rest for a minute. I'll wake you soon, we have time", he said, looking at his watch.

Standing in the middle of the street with his hood off, *Master Joe* clapped his metal hands painfully slow. Joe's future face looked as though it had been chewed off by a man-eating sea lion, regurgitated back into the ocean where is was eaten by fish which were caught and eaten by sailors, who then shat it out in a bad case of gastroenteritis. Serve that on a plate with eyeballs and a mouth and viola, *Master Joe*.

"Time travel has not been kind to you has it?" Joe yelled out coldly as Brandon's internal composition gave way, causing his body to slowly slide down the street light, splitting him in half and splashing onto the ground. Got to love a good ice breaker.

"Oh, so you think this is the end? HA! Every day I'll send more and more Cheese Sandwiches. No matter how many times your pathetic friends reset, you'll eventually be overrun!", *Master Joe* snarled, losing his usual calm demeanour which Joe picked up on immediately.

"You've gotta know by now that I can bypass the time loop effects? You know you're trapped in here with me just as much as I am with you. You're desperate to get out of here and it's written all over your ball-bag face. Even if we loop forever, I'll never let you have your freedom!"

Master Joe had no retort as he turned and pulled his hood back over his head, walking back down the empty street and kicking the occasional tin can like a little evil cry baby.

Closing the door, Joe turned around to see Bob back on his feet, peeking through the front lounge room window, concern had spread across his face from watching his future son and his present son locking horns.

"So, what's the plan now?" Bob asked, taking his blonde curly wig off and massaging his shoulders where the support bra was digging in.

"We go to war Dad. Again and again!"

Chapter Twelve
Joe's Diary

Day 1

I'm writing in this book which is being kept at Bob's caravan so that we know what happened, but none of us have to carry the burden of remembering it.

After Brandon and Aileen reanimated following the Cheese Sandwich ambush, we all left for the warehouse with two kilograms of prunes, thirty litres of water and a lot of memories. We memorized the literal shit out of us so that when we reset in the future, the last memory we have is today. Day 1 of our fight.

We're all bunkered down in the house now. Our memory tablet supply should last us about 31 days. Given the rate the Cheese Sandwiches multiply by, we are expecting to be overrun by day 27.

Bob counted sixteen Cheese Sandwiches at the last assault, plus the two that attacked me. If his calculations are correct, their numbers will double every day.

I hope he isn't right...

Hey, I'm back, what did I miss? Hmm let's see…

Day 2…boring.

Day 3…not much better.

Day 4, Aileen cleans her warts with Brandon's toothbrush. Good Lord, this is some bland material. Leave it with me and I'll find the good stuff!

Day 8

Bob's theory has stayed true so far. Today was a long day. Wave after wave of sandwiches crashed on our reinforced front door as soon as the sun rose. In the aftermath, we counted over two thousand slain sandwiches. Most of them were held at bay with makeshift flamethrowers using Aileen's extensive collection of Vagi-Spray aerosols, which she insists she bought by accident thinking it was deodorant.

Fortunately, our supplies replenish each night, but we barely made it through today with what we had, and they breached two windows near the lounge room.

It's also true that the cheese which holds them together is getting weaker. However, they still put up a ferocious fight, and by day 27 there will be over one billion of them…

We need to stick to our plan.

One billion cheese sandwiches? Holy constipation that's a lot of cheese. I'm flabbergasted. So flabbergasted that if my flab were to flib or flob, it would flabble me into a flibbly flobble of ghastement. The English language is broken. Get over it.

Day 13

So many sandwiches...so...many. We heaped their bodies into lots of a thousand each and counted over sixty thousand sandwiches before another wave broke through just after sunset.

It was a good choice not to remember anything except for Day 1. I don't think I could handle the burden of that knowledge.

The sandwiches broke through the front door in their hundreds after midday, flattening Aileen underneath. By the time Brandon, Bob and I pushed them back she was flatter than the carpet.

Thank goodness she didn't die the way I read on day 11! I couldn't think of a death worse than being eaten alive by Cheese Sandwiches. How is that even possible?

On a good note, we've collected all the pigeons we could find in Doomsville and housed them over at the warehouse. Over nine hundred of them. Next step is on track. We just need to hold on.

Look at you Joe, all grown up with your story telling narration and not giving away too much detail like a pro. If I wasn't so bored, I'd be proud.

Day 19

How in the hell did they make a trebuchet? No sooner do we wake up, the Cheese Sandwiches are using siege tactics to get into the second floor of our house which is clearly our weak spot.

Then there was the cheese ram, the cheese Batista and their attempt at a cheese Trojan horse! They might be getting weaker individually, but now that they are in the millions it doesn't matter.

Brandon went upstairs to fortify the window and a cheese hook caught him in the shoulder, dragging him out the window and into a waiting horde below. They had a boiling pot ready to go and ceremonially lowered him inside. Once they'd boiled him alive, they catapulted his own body parts into our house.

Aileen shoved me into the cupboard under the stairs after a fresh wave broke through the front door in the afternoon. When I got out at 8pm, Aileen had been turned into a human wheel of cheese. Bob barely made it out alive. I'm afraid we won't make it much longer.

At least the little bastards are inventive. Human wheel of cheese? There is more irony in that statement than a piece of iron being ironed ironically, by an ironical iron made from iron.

Day 26

We're finally here. Although I can't remember any of the previous days, I feel exhausted.

We decided to use a funnel technique and hold out in the laundry. Their enormous numbers meant nothing there. We took it in turns to swing away at the six-foot-tall insurgence of millions of Cheese Sandwiches.

They came at us with toothpicks which they used for spears. Brandon literally died from a thousand small cuts.

Aileen started throwing her cats at the wall of sandwiches. Those brave bastards gave them hell.

She finally told me about what happened with her, the llama and the chopsticks. I never knew the human body could fit so much mercury in one orifice! Let alone the pressure she had from the Chinese gang lords to assassinate that famous panda on live television. I don't think I'll ever look at a llama the same way again. She is a remarkable woman.

> *We have everything we need. Now we'll do what Master Joe would never expect.*
>
> *We strike back!*

Why do I feel like that explanation about Aileen's llama and chopsticks incident raises more questions than answers? I'll get to the mercury filled bottom of that story one of these days.

•

Chapter Thirteen
The Final Countdown

We have arrived at our final destination, please remain seated until the book has come to a complete conclusion, epilogue skippers I'm looking at you, and make sure all emotional trays are stored away along with whatever shred of dignity you have left.

Huddled up together in the laundry like a group of penguins baring the cold, Bob's 4am alarm startled the group into a panicked state. Aileen's early morning bowel movements were set off, causing the rest of the group to slip and slide out of the laundry like an Olympic Bobsleigh team on a brown ice track.

"We have no time to waste", Bob spluttered as he leant on the kitchen bench drawing in deep breaths of fresh air, "They'll be at our door in less than two hours if we don't get ready."

Planning and rehearsing for this very moment every day for the past two weeks, turned the group into a well-oiled machine as they gathered their bags and makeshift weapons, setting out for the warehouse under the cover of pre-dawn darkness.

Lined up in their feathery battalions with two small leather straps on either side of their breasts and a small black pouch strapped on their back, this army of pigeons was hungry for battle. Every morning since the day they collected the carrier pigeons from abandoned aviaries around Doomsville, Bob tediously spent the early hours of the morning prior to sunrise teaching the group to hone-in on the sight of a Cheese Sandwich, incorporating extreme training tactics that would breach the Geneva Convention. But this is war, and in order to make a pigeon pie you have to crack a few pigeons...mentally.

"Their pouches contain a self-administering dose of a stomach-acid inducing explosive, timed to be administered directly into their stomachs via a fine needle which is linked to a transponder on our synchronised watches", Bob flashed his watch at the group as they all exchanged disapproving looks at his flagrant disregard for animal welfare.

"Guys, sacrifices must be made! They have their job today and we have ours", Bob implored, digging into a large black duffle bag and passing around the other watches and some new weapons he had been meddling with for this very occasion.

"No Joe, none for you", said Bob, grabbing the extendable toilet brush baton from Joe's hands and kneeling in front of him. "You have to do your part unimpeded. We have this handled. This is non-negotiable."

Joe nodded reluctantly and walked over to Brandon who was strapping two large brown ammunition belts across his chest in an 'X' shape, much like a machine gunner in the army. Instead of actual ammunition, he had dozens of cheese cracker grenades, sure to shred through even the mightiest of Cheese Sandwich warriors.

"Brandon, I want to tell you...", Joe began as Brandon pulled on his military black boots that Bob had lent him, tying a red band around his head which depicted an image of a cheese grater in the centre.

"...I don't know how to thank you for standing by me-", Joe stopped mid-sentence as tears began to well up. He didn't want this to be the last time he saw his best friend. Not after all they had been through.

Looking up after attaching his weapon of choice to his back, which Brandon referred to as the 'De-Brie Maker', he grabbed hold of Joe's shoulders with an enormous grin on his freckled young face.

"Dude, this has been the best and craziest time of my life. Am I scared? Hell yeah I am! But I know you won't give up on us today. What's the worst that could happen? You've already gotten me killed over a dozen times! Ha", Brandon jested as he embraced Joe with a tight bear hug, pushing back from him and wiping a tear from his eyes.

Joe walked over to Aileen who was holstering two electric drills on either side of her exceptionally large love handles, each drill piece was replaced with razor sharp egg beaters and additional drill batteries lined up all around her belt in magazine pouches. As she tied her thick and severely unwashed black mane up in a strict bun, Joe copped a lashing from her foot-long armpit hair.

"What's that cannon you have there?", Joe pointed to a large white tube about two meters long, which had bicycle tyres attached to the rear and a cat crate locked on top. A hatch lever dropped the crates contents into the tube, and at the rear there was a crude air compressor bolted on.

"Ah this is our artillery Joey boy", Aileen explained as she tried to re-adjust her rainbow coloured knitted sweater, tucking it into her stained and over worn pink tracksuit pants.

Inspecting the bustling warehouse for cannon balls

or any other forms of projectiles, Joe looked back to Aileen with intrigue.

"Ah, well I call it the 'Pussy Destroyer'. So, you can probably guess from the name what I'm going to use", Aileen chirped away.

Joe choked on his words, "Pussy Destroyer?", scrunching his face into a ball as he used all the mental might he could to not envisage what Aileen had just said, diverting his thoughts to his happy place of puppies, rainbows and…Pussy Destroyers?

"Arghhhh", screamed Joe as Aileen clipped his ear with her eagle claws for hands, piercing his lobe wide enough to fit a bottle cap inside.

"The cannon fires my pussy cats you perverted little man", scolded Aileen as she grabbed the rope attached to the cannon, towing it outside of the warehouse with another cable attached to a trailer holding the crates of Aileen's ferocious felines.

Rubbing his raw ear Joe smiled to himself, 'She must really love me if she is willing to sacrifice her cats'.

Loading the pigeon cages into the caravan and hitching it to his rusted 50's styled pickup truck, Bob donned his magnum opus of disguises. Dressed in a blue Scottish kilt which displayed those splendid calves again, Bob bared his bulging pectorals and thick black chest hair with a long brown wavy wig blowing majestically in the wind.

He was holding a broad shield in one hand, made from rows of toilet rolls reinforced with Joe's unwashed and impressively rigid socks, topped off with a layer of aluminium foil for theatrical appearance. In the other hand, a long sword that looked suspiciously like the prosthetic leg from under the dining table, covered in used shaver heads sharp enough to cut through Aileen's three-inch kneecap hair which is denser than a neutron star.

Applying blue war paint to half of his face, Bob caught Joe's concerned expression.

"Don't you worry about us. You just get to that abandoned mine shaft before the battle starts. We'll do the rest", Bob insisted, opening the tray to the pickup truck and letting Brandon and Aileen climb aboard with their array of barbaric weapons.

Cutting their long goodbyes short for the sake of good plot progression but terrible character development, Bob, Brandon and Aileen departed the warehouse in the rusted pickup, weighed heavily by the caravan and dragging like an old goat's testicles in the dirt.

Picking the darkest clothes his deceased godfather

had available, Joe thought he looked like a suave 'Double 0' agent with a license to kill. In reality, the black turtle neck was so large that Joe's head was in a constant struggle to not be engulfed in the foreskin shaped jumper, and the black pants he thought were military grade, were in fact Aileen's old pair of latex Dominatrix leggings. Stains included.

Walking in the opposite direction of the group and heading to the nearest mine shaft entrance, Joe steeled his nerves for the task ahead. Reaching into his pocket and whipping out some seriously outdated black sunglasses, he walked into the oncoming sunrise. Joe took this time to pun himself into cringeworld with some internal motivation, albeit in a low, gravely voice.

'I guess you could say its time…'

Don't you do it Joe!

'…to fix time'

You lame son of a bitch.

•

Driving erratically on the freshly dewed grass, Bob skidded to a halt nearing the middle of Doomsville Central Park, sending Aileen crashing onto Brandon in an image best described as a beached whale rolling onto an unsuspecting hermit crab.

Prying himself free from Aileen's breasts which had swung around his head like a saggy game of tetherball, Brandon pulled himself up onto the trucks roof to see what caused the sudden stop.

Covering the other half of Doomsville Central Park and stretching far out into the residential streets beyond, was a standing army of one billion Cheese Sandwiches in perfect battle formation. The front line consisted of basic infantry sandwiches with their sharpened breadstick spears pointing forward and domed Havarti helmets, revealing only their beady red eyes. Flanking on both sides were the heavy cavalry sandwiches riding on their delicious baguette horses covered in shiny Camembert armour. Bringing up the centre and rear were the cheesy Crossbowmen with their crouton hardened arrows guarding an assortment of Cheese Sandwich siege weapons.

A chant began as Bob exited the pickup truck, helping Brandon and Aileen out of the tray.

"SAY CHEESE! SAY CHEESE! SAY CHEESE!"

The ground shook as their tiny cheesy legs stamped on the spot in unison, pointing their weapons up in the air and back down with each syllable.

Unfazed by the sheer numbers and the deafening roars, Bob, Brandon and Aileen unpacked the weaponry and unhitched the caravan.

Standing on the rear tray of the pickup truck with his back to the sea of bread and cheese, the rising sun shone on Bob's freshly shampooed wig. He faced Brandon and Aileen and gave them the inspirational pre-battle speech we have all come to loath from action and war movies alike.

Holding his head high and proud Bob bellowed out, "Today we stand at the precipice. Our great town is once more threatened to crumble and topple into the sea of obscurity..."

"Precip-what?", whispered Brandon, receiving a sharp foot stomp from Aileen's throbbing bunions in response.

"...Doomsville – That word should have a new meaning for all of us today. We can't be consumed by out petty differences anymore...once again you will be fighting for our freedom, not from tyranny, oppression or Aileen's cooking – but from annihilation...", Bob paused for added effect before pacing up and down the truck with both arms behind his back.

"Ok, now I'm confused", admitted Aileen, turning away from Bob to tend to her 'Pussy Destroyer', lining it up and filling the holding crate with her prized but shabby cats.

"...And dying in your beds many years from now, would you be willing to trade that one chance, just one chance to come back here and tell our enemies that they may take our lives...", yelled Bob, fluctuating between an American and Scottish accent.

"LOOK OUT!", Brandon screamed, disrupting a copyright infringement at the crucial moment.

A large wheel of tasty vintage cheese slammed into the pickup truck, rocking it violently as it crumbled into a hundred pieces. Snapping out of his movie quoting binge, Bob raced into the driver's seat and started up the engine, signalling Brandon with his arm out the window.

"Let's do this!", Brandon screeched in excitement, taking his 'De-Brie Maker' off his back, which was just a leaf blower enhanced with a cylindrical lawn mower blade attached to the end. He ran to the caravan door and opened it. He was immediately blown backwards onto the ground by the thousand pigeons surging out and heading towards the battlefield.

Blowing on horns made from paper napkins, the Cheese Sandwich frontline and heavy cavalry broke ranks, charging forward as the large black Doomsville clock at the centre of the park struck

6am.

With his head out the driver's window and wielding his prosthetic leg-sword, Bob accelerated heavily towards the first wave of evil carbohydrates, thinking only of Joe as the squadron of ravenous pigeons blocked out the sun overhead and cats flew in arched trajectories in front of him with fangs and claws at the ready.

'This is for you my son', Bob told himself as his truck ploughed into the oncoming wave of certain death.

•

Locating the mine site entrance was the easy part for Joe. Navigating his way in the dark damp tunnels was more difficult than giving directions to a quadriplegic mole with advanced dementia, living in an upside-down mirror world.

Bumping and grinding his way through the increasingly claustrophobic chambers, Joe could hear the droll humming of a million war-raging yells many meters above him. The occasional explosion on the surface sent shock waves which threatened to break the tunnels supportive beams. He urged himself to keep moving, 'Don't let all of this be for nothing Joe. Come on man!'

In the back of his mind he knew the truth. This was

a one-way trip.

Even with the pigeons, they were still outnumbered one million to one. In the house they might have stood a chance but not out in the open.

And that was the beauty of the plan. It was doomed to fail so that *Master Joe* wouldn't suspect a thing. Waiting for the Cheese Sandwiches to reach the one billion mark was Joe's idea after seeing Bob tear the Cheese Sandwich apart with his bare hands.

If they could dilute the power of The Entity across enough minions, then maybe its focus would be so drawn away it might not notice a sneak attack at its heart. That was the theory anyway.

In what felt like an eternity, Joe looked down at his new digital watch Bob had given him, synchronized with identical ones Brandon and Aileen had, each with the ability to inject the pigeons for the coup d'état. But not before 7am. Joe needed enough time to get to the mine's centre.

6:48am

Joe's stress was rising like a stressed-out stress ball, watching the notoriously stressful horror film, "I know whose balls you squeezed last summer".

Clambering his way through the last leg of the tunnel, with more difficulty than a baby elephant caught midway through the birthing canal, Joe could finally see the path open up as the mine's heart came into view.

The other four mineshaft tunnels surrounding Doomsville intersected into a wide circular room, big enough to fit a small auditorium. Lit only with green lanterns hung in each quadrant, Joe carefully entered this house of pain.

As far as evil villain lairs go, it was nothing like what Joe had expected, but everything he should have feared.

Looking for a large church organ on top of a flight of stairs in the middle of the room?

How about I do one better and give you an organ made from actual organs! With every pipe made from dozens of human windpipes, two rows of keys made from severed fingers and a pedalboard with real feet for pedals! White polished femur bones hold the abomination upright, as a tight layer of lacquered flayed skin covers the external panels which are made up of interlocking adult sized rib cages. The seat even has real buttocks for cushions...yeah, he went there.

Oh, that didn't upset you? You've clearly been de-sensitized by all this mindless violence. Touché

Take a look to the left!

Oh no! It's a large multi-coloured seven-seater lounge made entirely from floppy puppy ears. It's possessed by a child eating demon who requires live sacrifices to be made daily in order to keep its cushions nice and plump.

Still not good enough? Ok then, take a look to the right!

Oh my! A bewitched stainless-steel fridge sits in the kitchen. It keeps live baby goats in the cooler and pricks their feet so that it can dispense the salty innocent tears for your evil refreshment.

Want more? Now look up!

Wondered where the noble citizens of Doomsville were all this time? Well wait no longer!

Hundreds of preserved puppet corpses are hanging from the ceiling locked into various positions. All have painted smiles on their faces and are dressed in cutesy clothes that make even the creepiest doll collector look sane by comparison.

But wait, there's more.

As Joe walked ever so closer to the organ of cadavers, the pipes suddenly came to life with a tune so pungent it made Mozart's farts sound like a requiem.

The fleshy tubes churned out blood and bile with each slow keynote as rows of puppet corpses began to descend from the ceiling then rise back up in alternating turns. Each puppet's arms and legs move in solemn dance poses as they fall downwards and dip their smiling faces to look at Joe, before rising back up to the ceiling.

Holding onto all the grit he had left, while ducking and diving through the many memorable faces of Doomsville, Joe made it to the set of steep stairs at the foot of the circular platform which held the organ. From his lowered position he could see a purple hue emanating from under the organ, pulsating with energy.

'The Entity! It must be', Joe foolishly thought to himself, as The Entity invaded his mind through telepathic powers and alerted *Master Joe* of his presence.

Ceasing the putrid pipe organ song, *Master Joe* spoke directing to the purple light, "What? He's here? Why couldn't you sense him earlier?!"

Making his way up the stairs to the rear of the organ, Joe could hear *Master Joe* scurry back and forth on the platform in a panic, seemingly talking to himself, but Joe knew he must have a telepathic connection to The Entity.

Lifting the skin edging to the organ, Joe saw the rare alien rock seated underneath, no bigger than a medium sized dog, and glowing with an aura of pure purple energy.

'Gotchya', Joe spoke directly to The Entity, feeling its presence.

Casually walking around to the side, Joe caught *Master Joe* slowly turning around, hood down and ugly up.

"Now I had you pegged for something far smarter than this my child. But this is delicious none the less", said *Master Joe*, taking a seat on his rambunctiously buttocked chair, which let off a small squeak causing *Master Joe* to inconspicuously look around for a farting frog.

"How did I turn out to be such a wanker?", spat Joe, leaning on the organ and flicking a human finger key with as much cold indifference as he could muster.

Gritting his teeth in frustration, *Master Joe* leant forward, pointing his metal digit at Joe's head, "As titillating as it might be to enter into another table tennis match of words with you, young and naive one, I would much rather tell you how poorly your friends are doing up there. They'll never be reset after today! My sweet Entity will make sure their last moments are the most sufferable they have ever had"

"You think so little of yourself", Joe said with an unusual amount of conviction, "I wouldn't come all this way to save my friends. They know this is their last day. Do you know this is yours?"

Without waiting for *Master Joe*'s witty but completely predictable reply, Joe reached under the organ and placed a hand on the alien rock. A surge of corrosive energy pierced his brain, soothing and torturing him at the same time.

"Hahah! This is too delightful. You think you can control The Entity and use it against me? I'm the only one that can! It bonded with meeeee!", shouted *Master Joe* as he gingerly stood up from his seat, raising one eyebrow and cocking his repugnant head to the side as he watched Joe.

With purple light poring out of his black eyes, Joe turned to his now horrified older self, "Oh but I can. I'm you after all"

•

Bob made it only twenty meters into the thick swarm of murderous meals, before the cheese from the vanquished sandwiches seeped into the front grill of the truck and seized the engine.

Battling his way back up to the caravan using long sweeps of his leg sword and shielding himself from hot cheese fondue being slung from trebuchets, Bob watched Brandon and Aileen fight valiantly up ahead, clearing his path with a combination of precise cat launches and cheese cracker grenades.

Pigeons were diving in and out of the ever-growing mass of snacks, pecking with such a fury which left even the strongest sandwich in crumbs.

Aileen was now brandishing her rolling pin nun chucks, sending dozens of sandwiches flying with each crushing blow. Forming a tight three-man triangle with their backs to one another they swung, bashed, lunged, parried, thrusted, decapitated and disembowelled the relentless sandwiches who now encircled them.

"I think now is a good time Bob...", panted Brandon, as he swept his 'De-Brie' maker in semi-circles ahead of him, sending cheesy limbs flying, "...my batteries are dying"

"Take these my boy", Aileen passed Brandon the nun chucks behind her back as she duel-wielded her egg beater drills, "He's right Bob. We need to do it now!"

Shield charging a unit of heavy cavalry sandwiches, Bob looked up to the Doomsville clock.

6:52am

"Eight more minutes! We have to give him all the time we can-", pleaded Bob, interrupted by Aileen's scream of surprise from behind.

"You son of a burger!", yelled Aileen as her legs were lassoed by hundreds of cheesy ropes, bringing her to her callous ridden knees, with hundreds more lasso's tying her arms, pulling her hands closer to her chest and face, locking the drills she was holding onto their highest setting.

Unable to break their formation, Bob was forced to watch in his peripheries as Aileen struggled against the increasing strength of the cheese bondage. One sharpened egg beater began to dig its way millimetre by millimetre into her chest cavity, while the other beater was transforming her face into a mangled Aileen-omelette. Some would say it's an improvement.

For three gruelling minutes the egg beaters minced their way through flesh and bone until Aileen's screams of agony turned into soft gurgles.

Now back to back, Brandon and Bob gave it everything they had. They climbed onto the roof of the caravan with millions of sandwiches clambering up its sides in a pyramid of problematic proportions.

Riding on the back of a hijacked pigeon above, a kamikaze sandwich dived onto Brandon's shoulders, it pulled the pins out of all the remaining cheese cracker grenades he had on his belt before Brandon managed to swat it away.

If you have Pavarotti's song 'Nessun Dorma', now would be the time to play it. I'll wait.

With a single tear dripping down the side of his face, Brandon looked to Bob and smiled. Bob's eyes welled up as he nodded back in respect to his good friend.

Arms outstretch, Brandon leaned back off the edge of the caravan like the metaphorically crucified martyr he was.

As the ocean of eagerly awaiting sandwiches on the ground engulfed his body, the grenades detonated.

Cheese cracker shrapnel flew out faster than the speed of sound in a fifty-meter radius, impaling thousands of sandwich warriors. The shock wave came soon after, breaking tens of thousands of sandwiches apart instantaneously, rocking the caravan onto its side with Bob barely hanging on to the edge with one arm.

Much like throwing a large rock from a great height into an overflowing toilet bowl, Brandon's liquefied innards and detached extremities flew tens of meters into the air and splashed back down onto the caravan.

Arduously dragging himself on top of the upturned caravan, Bob looked out across the now silent and heavily fogged battlefield. For a moment he felt at peace. But that moment faded fast as the fog cleared and he saw millions more sandwiches standing fast around the circular debris of their fallen comrades.

Falling onto his back in pure exhaustion, Bob angled his head to see the pigeons still fighting the good fight, popping in and out with a speed too fast to be caught. Even with their veracity, they were barely making a dent.

The napkin horns blew for a last time as the Cheese Sandwiches mounted their final charge. Pressing down the activation button on his digital watch as it flashed red with a ten second countdown, Bob closed his eyes and called the pigeons to him with a small silver whistle.

9 seconds

The sandwiches made their way up onto the caravan, crawling up Bob's legs.

5 seconds

Tying down all his limbs, the sandwiches carried up

a circular saw and turned it on between his legs, edging it closer with devious grins.

1 second

Centimetres away from a certain nutcracker demise, the sandwiches stopped to look up in awe as the thousand cooing birds descended on the caravan.

0 seconds

Feathers and fire were the last things Bob ever saw.

•

An enormous shockwave from the explosion above sent the grotesque pipe organ tumbling down the stairs, crashing into pieces and leaving only the alien rock, Joe and *Master Joe* sprawled out on the platform.

Temporarily broken from his trance with The Entity, Joe looked at his flashing red watch and felt a surge of pluckiness inject into his very heart. With all his might he begged The Entity to bind with him, like it did with *Master Joe*. He could feel its confusion as it agreed with his request, unable to distinguish which Joe was which. It's only weakness.

Almost at a full connection with The Entity, Joe looked at *Master Joe*'s deeply concerned face as he heard the grave news from his last remaining Cheese Sandwiches on the surface.

"I knew I couldn't kill you", Joe began to monologue, as *Master Joe* got to his feet looking wildly around for his reinforcements who were inevitably making their way through the mine shaft tunnels.

"Well, you got one thing right today my child", spat *Master Joe*, crossing his arms and staring manically at Joe's hand on The Entity, "Doesn't matter what your little friends did, I still have enough minions to overpower you!"

Joe knew *Master Joe* couldn't interfere with his connection to The Entity even if he wanted to. Paradox 101.

Light from little breadstick torches were making their way closer in each of the five tunnels surrounding him, pushing Joe to take the next step.

"So instead of killing you, how about I kill us instead!", Joe said, willing The Entity with all his concentration to take him back to the year 2002, the night of his conception.

"YOU WOULDN'T DARE!", cried *Master Joe*, diving onto the alien rock as Joe disappeared before his eyes.

18th SEPTEMBER 2002: 8PM

If any children are reading this, unless you've had the 'Birds and the Bees' speech, please give this book to your parents. While you're at it, maybe call child protective services for them letting you read this book in the first place!

Joe's world turned to white before being plunged into an enormous game of Tetris, with buildings and scenery plummeting down from above, locking into place and becoming the past.

Appearing right before him was his old house. The Brown family home. No longer under a biohazard dome, it wore fresh white paint on its walls and a brilliant shade of red on the roof.

A shiver of excitement raced down Joe's spine as he watched the lounge room light turn on, which he quickly quelled, reminding himself of his true intentions. 'This is bigger than you Joe! Plus, they won't even know you exist yet'.

Creeping up to the window with more creep than a creepy creeper vine stalking a lonely botanist, Joe watched the much younger and more virile versions of his parents play fight in the kitchen while dancing to music.

'I've missed you Mum', thought Joe, holding back

his emotions as best he could.

Bob was much skinnier and less barrel chested then the Bob Joe was used to, with black hair in a crew cut style and a well-groomed beard of his own, wearing a red flannelette shirt and skinny black jeans.

Joe's mother, Quinn, had long blonde hair and piercing blue eyes, standing only slightly shorter than Bob with a curvy physique and wearing high waist jeans with a white singlet. Neither could have been over twenty years old at the time.

Before he knew it, Joe had been watching both of them for over an hour in a haze of sweet nostalgia.

With things heating up between the two in the kitchen, Joe had the feeling that it was getting close to intervene. Even just delaying the conception one day could result in him never being born.

He tried to avert his eyes, but he'd never seen butter being used in that peculiar way.

The things they did with the corking screw had Joe questioning his beliefs. And don't even get me started with the way Quinn worked that spatula around with the egg rings tightened in a karma sutra styled lock.

It got hotter and hotter. Sweat dripping off Bob's

nose as he beat it faster, pounded it harder. Quinn moaned and groaned as she struggled to fit it in but sighed loudly in relief as they finished the job.

It was unmistakable.

They had just made the best God damn lemon meringue Joe had ever seen.

Sneaking past the window to the front door, Joe observed a long red transparent tube of energy tethered to his body flowing out of his chest and into the house.

As he touched this glowing tube, Joe knew exactly what it was. It showed him all the decisions and all the paths taken to get to his future in a split second of blinding information. If he concentrated hard enough, he could see a million more tubes shining out of the houses all around, the paths of everyone's past moving forward into the future.

This is how *Master Joe* knew exactly what to manipulate in the past to get what he wanted in the future. He had tapped into the quantum memory of space-time itself.

Joe flicked a nearby ladybug off a leaf and watched its tubed path change from red to blue, indicating a new path and a new future. Possibly a path of revenge on Joe for flicking it. Don't underestimate the tenacity of a scorned ladybug!

Ringing the doorbell, Joe nervously waited at the front door, not sure how he truly felt about his next course of action.

Bob answered the door in a huff while pulling his pants back on. Joe knew he got there just in time.

Bob stared at Joe with a blank expression, but he didn't give Bob the chance to speak.

Winding up and kicking harder than a frightened mule at an illegal 'Donkey Show', Joe felt his ancestors cry out loud as his foot sent Bob's testicles into the back of his throat.

Running from the door, Joe looked at his hands expecting them to fade away or dissolve into nothingness. Anything to indicate he was ceasing to exist.

Joe stopped under a broken streetlight a few hundred meters down the road, hands on his knees as he drew in some deep breaths. 'What the hell! There's no way they finished the…job after that!', Joe pondered, frustration clawing at his mind.

"Oh, bravo my child…Bravo", whispered *Master Joe* from behind the streetlight, walking past Joe and into the middle of the dimly lit street.

"I enjoy delivering pain as much as the next person,

but to do that to our father was simply...NUTS! I never knew you had the...BALLS to do it! Haha", laughed *Master Joe*, thrilled at his childish jokes.

Clenching his fists into sweaty balls, Joe searched his red tube of energy for any change to the timeline but failed to see anything significant.

"Hmm, using the quantum memory network I see", *Master Joe* stated, walking in tight spirals around Joe, "Well if you looked hard enough, you'll see that I predicted you would return tonight, so I travelled back a month earlier!"

Frowning so hard his forehead bared a close resemblance to a cockroach's rectum, Joe could see the day *Master Joe* arrived.

"Extracting mothers' eggs in her sleep was the easy part. Finding a cloning facility to splice our genome into it was a little tedious to say the least", *Master Joe* quipped, enthralled by Joe's defeated appearance.

"Sneaking in to implant the fertilized egg was a synch. Sure, we might be born a day or two earlier, but the overall change that makes is inconsequential! Mwahahah", cackled *Master Joe*, clasping his metal hands over his mouth and jumping up and down excitedly, his head bobbing around like a perverted lava lamp.

Let's not stop to dwell too much on the philosophical implications of a son impregnating his own mother through artificial insemination. I'm sure there's been enough written about that kind of Freudian disorder. Does he have to gouge his eyes out now or later? I forget.

Without hesitation, Joe reached into the quantum memory network and travelled further back to his Grandfather before Bob was born. *Master Joe* beat him to it.

He travelled back to his great-great-Grandmother's wedding day. *Master Joe* was the flower girl.

Frustrated, Joe travelled as far back as his great-great-great-Grandfather's best friends cousin's bar mitzvah. *Master Joe* was the Rabbi.

Mentally exhausted from tapping into his ancestry, Joe sat in the white nothingness of the space-time void, clearing his mind in meditation. *Master Joe* knew he would attack his own lineage directly and was well prepared. Joe needed to think outside the box and do something so unpredictable that *Master Joe* couldn't see it coming.

Immerging into the void, *Master Joe* floated over Joe narrowing his black eyes at his younger self, "As much as I have been amused by our little escapades my child, I do wonder. How exactly have you made it this far? You couldn't have done all of this alone..."

Scratching his chin with his metal fingers as Joe immersed himself in the quantum memory network, *Master Joe* gazed directly at me, your humble narrator.

"YOU! You're the reason why he's made it this far! You've been helping him all along!", screeched the paranoid and delusional *Master Joe*, clearly mistaking me for someone else.

"Oh, I'm not mistaken, you son of a shaved snake's scrotum!", hissed *Master Joe*, reaching past the safety of my fourth wall and clasping his metal hand over my neck...

Cough

Splutter

Gasp

I...can't...breathe

I...can't...actually be strangled! I have no neck HA! Jokes on you Master Mammary Head.

"You're going to stop helping Joe or so help me, I'll find your son Little Timmy who narrates children's pop-up books, and when I'm done with him, the only thing he will narrate after that will be his own...EULOGY!", shrieked *Master Joe* as he slipped back into the storyline.

Holy assless chaps of Valhalla!

I'm sorry guys, gals and invertebrates, I can't help anymore, you're on your own. My imaginary son is all I have.

I'll still describe, belittle and berate for you of course, but you have to get Joe to the end now.

Unaware of *Master Joe*'s blatant breach of the International Narrator Protection Act of 1901, Joe gloved up for the fight of his life, locating the most obscure connections to his existence throughout history. But where to strike first? That's entirely up to you, the simple-minded reader.

•

TIME TRAVEL BATTLE ROYALE!

It's a three round, 5th dimensional fight to the death.

The rules of the fight are simple. Choose how you, the reader, want to beat this bobble headed freak into oblivion. Help Joe pick his destinations one at a time, and metaphorically knock *Master Joe* on his righteous Gluteus Maximus.

Let's make like Quasimodo at one of his unhealthy sanctuary orgies and ring the proverbial bell. Ding ding.

ROUND ONE

1)   Find and kill a pet chicken named Dorothy in the south province of France, 1789. – go to p236

2)   Attend Roswell, New Mexico in 1947 to hi-jack a crashed UFO. – go to p238

INTERUPT AN ANCIENT SABERTOOTH TIGER HUNT, RUSSIA 56,100 BCE

Stalking a great and mighty Saber-tooth tiger through the frost-bitten wilderness of Central Russia, Joe could barely believe the size of this legendary creature making its way through the dense snow-capped hills.

Hiding in a large hollowed out tree, Joe watched the early Homo sapien tribal leader crouch low and aim his long spear with intense precision. Using a freshly plucked Dodo feather attached to a long branch, Joe tickled the nose of the hunter as he wound up for the throw, ditching the spear up in the air and landing next to the now enraged killer Saber-tooth tiger, chasing the hunter off the edge of a cliff and into the frozen lake below.

Joe waited and waited.

Nothing happened.

You really thought stopping the culling of one extinct mammal fifty thousand years ago was going to have a significant impact on the future? Clearly you haven't read the other option...

1)   Displace a migrating Dung beetle near the River Nile, Egypt 3004 BCE. – go to p240

'ET TU, BRUTUS?' 15 MARCH 44BCE

Setting himself up as Julius Caesars wine servant for the better part of a year, Joe paid Brutus a dozen silver coins to take his place in the ultimate betrayal. As he plunged the last dagger into Julius' Caesars back, he forever changed the renowned phrase to, "Et tu, Joe?"

Fast forward to the first performance of 'The Tragedy of Julius Caesar' by William Shakespeare on 21 September 1599 at the Bankside Theatre in London. A heavily intoxicated but unknown female in history was watching the show with unique anticipation. She had recently come to the knowledge that her estranged husband, also named Joe, was having an affair. When the actor playing Julius cried out his betrayal by Joe in the final scene, it stabbed too at this woman's fragile heart. Leaving the theatre in a drunken rage, she travelled home where she killed her husband in his sleep.

On the day of the funeral, an unfortunate grave digger slipped in the wet conditions and fell into the open grave site, snapping his neck and dying instantly. He was the great ancestor of George Washington Carver, the co-inventor of peanut butter in 1890. Without George, peanut butter wouldn't be invented until many decades later, preventing Harry Burnett Reese from creating the beloved Peanut Butter Cups in 1928.

In a secret known only to a handful of intelligence services around the world, Peanut Butter Cups were what set off the cold war between Russia and America post 1947. President Truman met with Stalin to commence peace talks and brought these delicious treats as an offering. The highly allergic

Stalin took this as an attempt on his life and thus began the space arms race.

Without this epic event in history, man never conquered the moon on 21 July 1969, which for Joe's Grandfather was the catalyst for the day he and his Grandmother locked lunar lips after the landing and conceived Joe's father.

Meanwhile, back in the void of time-space, *Master Joe* frantically watched the ripples from 44 BC make their way at the speed of light towards the future, some two thousand years away. Not able to predict which path they would take, *Master Joe* did the best he could. He infiltrated the Kremlin in 1949 and assassinated Stalin with a Peanut Butter Cup to the eye.

The cold war began a lot hotter than before. America still won the space race in 1969. And Joe's father was born, albeit in a more dangerous world.

Joe sat in the white void and watched as *Master Joe* patched the timeline here and stemmed the space-time bleeds there. But it wasn't enough. Joe's quantum memory network tunnel turned amber to green. Just one step away from blue and diverging into a new path altogether.

Squeezing his eyes shut like Stalin's anaphylactic eye, Joe found the last roll of the dice at the very edge of human history.

1)   Displace a migrating Dung beetle near the River Nile, Egypt 3004 BCE. – go to p240

2)   Cause an early Homo sapien hunter to sneeze while they stalk a Saber-tooth tiger in Russia, 56,100 BCE. – go to p232

A CHICKEN NAMED DOROTHY, FRANCE 1789

Spending the better part of three months interrogating half the nation's chicken population, Joe had plucked, feathered and tarred his way to Dorothy's location. Sneaking into the golden plated coop, Joe found the chicken referred to as France's Poultry Princess.

A secret lost to history, Dorothy was Napoleon Bonaparte's closest confidant. Her clucks were rumoured to solve even the greatest of conundrums. After receiving her head in a box just days before the French Revolution got into full swing, a manic Napoleon returned to Paris almost ten years earlier than he would have.

Taking a personal vendetta against all guillotine executions that reminded him of his sweet Dorothy, Napoleon prevented the death of King Louis XVI at the hands of the smelly masses.

How did this snail loving frog of a King change the future? He didn't. But his monarchy remained intact and with-it Napoleon conquered the known world by 1821, throwing the world into a permanent state of croissant eating sleazebags.

World War I and II never happened because the French army now had a spine. Joe never lost his great uncle Tony at the battle of Normandy in 1944, which resulted in Tony changing his name to Tanya, adopting three children and living her life out as a housewife. Those children became famous oil tycoons and bought up all the land Doomsville was meant to be founded on in 1981. No Doomsville, no Joe. Or so he thought.

Unable to locate Dorothy before Joe did, *Master Joe* settled for impersonating King Louis XVI, redirecting Napoleons rage and repairing as much damage to the timeline as he could.

Joe watched his quantum memory network turn from red to amber, indicating he had changed his history and moved it closer to blue, but not quite enough.

Finding his Zen like a Taoist Grandmaster in a death metal mosh pit, Joe focused on the even more obscure branches further back in history that lead to his extinction.

ROUND 2

1)   Perform an exorcism on the Pope Urban II before the First Crusade in 1095 CE. - go to p239

2)   Take Brutus' place in stabbing Julius Caesar in the back, 15 March 44 BCE. - go to p233

ROSWELL, NEW MEXICO 1947

Joe beats the US National Guard to the crash site and using a pair of toenail clippers he takes the only surviving alien hostage, forcing it to restart the dish shaped UFO and take him to the mothership lying just outside the Asteroid belt. Before arriving, Joe throws the alien out of the airlock and pretends to be a peace offering sent from Earth to the noble and ancient race of aliens named the Zigglebottoms.

Joe spends the next twenty years rising to the rank of High Ambassador to Earth, bearing several thousand hybrid offspring that all look like a salamander crossed with a chimpanzee. When his political influence grew to a crucial level, Joe led an uprising on an intergalactic scale and overthrew the Zigglebottom Government. Commanding the imperial fleet, Joe returned to Earth on the year of his dad's birth to abduct him as a baby.

Unfortunately for Joe, *Master Joe* smuggled himself on the spacecraft in 1947 and spent the last twenty years disguised as Joe's alien breeding partner, which fortunately required no physical interaction thanks to their advances in technology. I continue to underestimate how emotionally disturbed *Master Joe* truly is…

Broadcasting the footage of Joe throwing the alien out of the air lock across the entire Zigglebottom Armada, *Master Joe* undermines Joe's mission to Earth, labelling him an outlaw. Hiding away in the furthest corners of the Andromeda Galaxy, the now fugitive Joe decides to go back and choose a different path.

1)   Find and kill a pet chicken named Dorothy in the south province of France, 1789. – go to p236

EXORCISM OF POPE URBAN II 1095

Disguising himself as an Archbishop, Joe infiltrated the Council of Clermont before Pope Urban II could call for the First Crusade. Claiming to have damning knowledge that involved the Pope, the hot summer of 1093 in Florence and a pagan goat, Joe created enough chaos to leverage a vote amongst the sermon to exorcise the Pope of his demons. During the exorcism, Joe uses his renowned ventriloquist skills to pretend to be the Popes demon, demanding the Roman Catholic Church outlaw seafood products or face eternity in hell.

The crusades were swapped with the Great Krill War of 1123, the barbaric Salmon Slaughter in 1389 and who could forget the unspeakable Battle of Octopus Hill in 1790. The ripple of change nearly made it to Joe's family seafood business in 1850, almost altering his destiny forever.

But before the wave of change crashed on Joe's ancestors, *Master Joe* sent himself back to 1 BCE. After killing Joseph of Nazareth and taking his place as Jesus' mentor, he created a whole new book of 'Joe', dedicated to insatiably holy seafood delights.

The ripple subsided, causing only minor changes to the future timeline, including a fanatic cult of Cristian Merfolk who lived underground, occasionally raiding the surface to wage fishy genocide on the mammalian scum. Otherwise Joe was left to rethink his decision.

1)   Take Brutus' place in stabbing Julius Caesar in the back, 15 March 44 BCE. – go to p233

DUNG BEETLE DISPLACEMENT, RIVER NILE EGYPT, 3004 BCE

Rolling its neat ball of camel dung in the hot midday sun, Joe moves the scarab three inches to the left and walks away. The scarab follows its doomed path into the River Nile, clinging desperately to its stinky portable home. Blasted out northward into the Mediterranean Sea, the poor beetle and its dung are swallowed whole by a young hammerhead shark.

The shark is caught in the net of a Greek fisherman and taken back to a small and ancient Athens where it gave the entire Town Council a fatal case of diarrhea. A series of tales from this event were written and then re-written by Aristotle who now drew his inspiration away from scriptures about logic, and instead wrote the infamous philosophical headscratcher, 'Anus: Where life ends, and chaos begins'.

A thirteen-year-old pimple faced Isaac Newton lines up to buy the outlawed metaphysical book in 1655 and is consequently beheaded soon after for it being in his possession. Ironically having his head decapitated in a public forum and falling into a basket didn't prompt any theories of gravity.

Flat Earthers paved the way up until the late 1800's without the influence of Newton's findings to counteract them, punishing any naysayers by reducing their once spherical shaped heads into pancakes with the use of an anvil, in a capital punishment sentence referred to as 'The Flattening'.

Even after the cultist's were disbanded, the damage

to the steel and iron industry was long standing. Anvil statues and anvil 'Flatteners' had taken up a large portion of the world's iron supply in the late 1890's, preventing all plans for an epic ship to be built. The Titanic.

Of the 1,517 people that should have died on its maiden voyage in 15 April 1912, it was the cook's assistant who lived on past their due date and went on to create a culinary dish known as the Fire of Hades. A soup so hot it killed thirty percent of its clientele, forcing a legal waiver to be signed prior to digesting its liquid magma of mayhem.

One of those brave souls was Joe's great-great-aunties personal gardener, kicking the spicy bucket before completing the annual firebreak around Joe's ancestor's home in Sicily. That year, a record heatwave broke through the country, setting the land alight and causing Joe's great-great-Grandfather to run into the house to save his sister, causing him to perish in the fire.

Wow…That's a bit of a stretch don't you think?

You're expected to believe that moving a dung beetle three inches off its path five thousand years ago caused Newton to die, a head flattening cult to rise, the Titanic never to sail and the death of Joe's lineage because of a hot soup that should have never existed? No wonder some people think science fiction is a poor man's non-fiction!

Stumped again by this ridiculous sequence of events, *Master Joe* scrambled to put out the space-time spot fires from Joe's timeline tampering. Unable to intervene until the very last moment, *Master Joe* bribed the local Sicilian police to block off all roads leading to his great-great-aunties property, preventing his great-great-Grandfather from courageously and somewhat foolishly attending the scene.

Falling to his knees in the white void that separates space from time, Joe was incapable of fathoming this massive timeline reversal. The once green quantum memory network teetering on turning blue and ready to eradicate Joe from the history of the universe, flicked back to red.

Everything Joe had done was reversed. Everything you just read for nothing. Everything.

Want a refund? Too late.

Maybe you should travel back in time and just avoid this book altogether. Who knows, instead of reading this pile of manure, you might have found the cure for cancer, resolved world poverty or knitted a nice jumper for your cat.

•

With a face more flushed than a clogged toilet, *Master Joe* hobbled over to Joe in the void, exhausted by his efforts but grinning smugly none the less.

"Give up my child. That was a brilliant effort I'll give you that much, but don't let it get to your head...that's my job! Mwahahah", screeched *Master Joe*, clutching his chest as he struggled to breathe through his own laughter.

Wiping away the oncoming stream of tears, Joe closed his eyes one last time and furrowed his brow with intensity, apologizing to the universe for his next time jump.

Concerned with Joe's newly founded confidence, *Master Joe* paced around him like a predatory piece of pizza targeting an overfed bulimic.

"I wouldn't bother trying to go back! Once you pulled that Egypt stunt, I sent millions of me's back in time, all throughout human history!", cried *Master Joe* as Joe began to disappear before him.

Joe extended both middle fingers at *Master Joe* as he turned transparent and slipped back into the space-time vortex.

Stopping in his tracks, *Master Joe*'s colour drained

from his face.

"He's going outside of human history...", he whispered out loud and disappeared into the vortex after Joe.

•

Standing on the shores of an interconnected continent near the equator some 385 million years ago, Joe watched in amazement as the very first fish to emerge from the ocean landed on the smooth rocks from the violent sea it had evolved in.

"Life on Earth will be better without us", said Joe, stroking the fish's blue slimy head as it inhaled air for the first time. Its four finned legs struggled to drag itself up onto the rock overlooking the onshore lake beyond, where it would lay its newly evolved eggs which were destined to bring humanity into existence in the far future.

Blasting face-first onto the rock just a few metres away, *Master Joe* jumped to his feet and dusted himself off. He pointed at Joe. Then at the fish. And finally, back at Joe.

"YOU WOULDN'T! THIS IS MAD, EVEN FOR ME!", *Master Joe* yelled, his voice breaking in high pitches under the stress.

Making peace with himself and the cosmos, Joe

smiled at his future self with pity.

"Humanity won't be missed. You've shown me how far evil is willing to go. I have to go further. Tell The Entity he needs to find another planet!"

"You son of a glazed ham-", *Master Joe* yelled, diving at Joe's legs in desperation as Joe drop-punted the fish thirty metres in the air and into the mouth of a waiting prehistoric shark.

Turning back around, Joe watched both versions of himself break down into cubes of information and then into prisms of energy, like a kaleidoscope of peaceful destruction. *Master Joe* screamed in agony as he folded into himself, but all Joe felt was relief.

'You did the right thing', were the last word's Joe said to himself as his whole world faded into a black abyss.

•

Waking from his dreamless sleep, Joe Brown stretched his extremities and …Oh come on! You're seriously not going to start this again? I don't get paid enough to narrate this. Wait a minute…I don't get paid at all!

Joe heard a voice echo from outside his room.

"Breakfast is ready Joe"

It wasn't Aileen's voice. And this wasn't Aileen's house. Joe spun around to find himself in his old room, full of all his old stuff that I have no intention of describing to you, but you can imagine!

Sprinting out of his bedroom like a retired racehorse galloping from the glue factory, Joe tore down the corridor and into the dining room. Sitting in their chairs at the small four-seater table and looking up at Joe like a picture-perfect family, was Bob and Quinn. Aged a good twenty years since he last saw them in 2002, but they were without a doubt his parents.

Joe squeezed his way in between his mother and father and wrapped an arm around each, dragging them in together so all three heads touched.

Giving Quinn an awkward glance, Bob gently pushed Joe off and straightened his chair, raising one eyebrow, "Alright son that's enough. What do you want?"

"Don't think this gets you out of Aileen's famous breakfast!", said Quinn, leaning back and frowning at Joe as if he'd let off a silent but deadly odour.

"Aileen?", squealed Joe in excitement, turning around to see the haggard old bag of skin hobbling over from the kitchen with food that looked somewhat edible.

"What in the bloody hell has gotten into you boyo?", said Aileen, swatting off Joe's attempt to bear hug her as she placed a pile of bacon in the middle of the table.

With all eyes locked onto him, it dawned on Joe. "None of you remember?"

"All I remember is you went to bed a grouch and woke up a gentleman", said Quinn, getting up from her chair and giving Joe a hug he had long forgotten.

'I don't know how this happened, but I don't care', Joe told himself as he gave into the soothing embrace.

DING DONG

The doorbell broke up the otherwise perfect moment, startling Joe as he looked for the nearest sharp implement.

"Woah son, easy now it's just Brandon. You invited him for breakfast yesterday, remember?", questioned Bob, looking at Quinn and shrugging his shoulders as he walked to the front door.

Sure enough, Brandon walked through the door with that enormous grin he always wore, shaking Bob's hand and giving Quinn a peck on the cheek.

"Oh man am I glad to see you again dude!", said Joe ecstatically, grabbing Brandon by both shoulders and shaking him in ways that would ordinarily get you imprisoned if it were a baby.

Looking to Bob and Quinn for help, Brandon stiffened up like a rigid possum playing dead near a powerline, "Chill out dude, I only saw you last night"

"Pay no attention to him Brandon my boy, he woke up a little loopy this morning", Aileen exclaimed, slapping down another plate on the table, but this time it was a tower of golden-brown buttered toast.

They sat and ate and laughed for hours, Joe was quiet for the most part, soaking it all up like a sponge at a murder scene.

Bob looked at his watch and with a shocked expression stared at Joe.

"What? What's wrong?!", Joe leapt up from his chair and adopted the crane pose, causing Brandon to choke on his toast and Aileen to fall off her chair in laughter.

"Jeez son, it's only a date. I was going to tell you you're running late for the movie", said Bob, scrunching up his face with bemusement.

"A date?", asked Joe, slowly making his way back to his seat as Aileen gave Brandon the Heimlich manoeuvre, which would have helped him if her saggy and unbridled breasts weren't bludgeoning him with each squeeze.

"Roxanne, you idiot!", yelled Brandon, coughing up the piece of toast and moving as far away from Aileen's barbaric bosoms as possible.

Ecstasy swept over Joe once more. This was it. The perfect life. His gamble paid off. He has his family, his friends and now his sweet innocent, totally going to be his girlfriend and there is nothing suspicious about any of this, Roxanne.

Joe promised himself when the day came for Doomsville to crumble away and wither, he wouldn't take the path *Master Joe* did.

'Yes, today's gonna be a good day', thought Joe as he walked away from the reader for the last time, jumping up with both feet, fist punching the air and clicking his heels together.

And he was right.

•

Sweet tarantulas' testicles that was a beautiful ending.

An ending so good it leaves the reader no reason to continue.

No reason to ruin the serendipitous moment that

will warm the cockles of even the coldest hearts.

Absolutely no point in destroying the memory of Joe by reading the Epilogue and forever bringing unspeakable guilt into your already debauched minds.

Oh, so you want to read it do you? Have you put on your big adult diapers and are ready for an uncontrollable flood of sadness to fill them to the brim?

You are the reason we can't have nice things in life.

Fine, see if I care. Just make sure when you read it, you're sitting on the toilet. That way you won't know what stinks worse. You, or the ending.

You've been warned!

EPILOGUE

Plunging the last of the sedatives into the intravenous tube, a black gloved hand places a syringe in a metal tray near a large glass jar.

The convulsions ease as the matter inside lulls itself into calmness.

Placing a round metal lid on the jar and turning it gently, the other gloved hand caresses the jar lovingly. Positive thoughts emanate from the owner of the jar through to the matter inside. A bond between them that goes beyond the physical.

"There there. You were having a bad dream, that's all", soothes the voice of the owner.

Carrying the jar over to its marble podium enclosure with more care than a mother holding a new born, the owner plants a kiss on the jar and closes the semi-circle glass domed lid over the podium.

The matter bobs up and down in its own tranquil blue sea as its original colour slowly returns.

"Ahh, there we go. That's the colour I love to see. You're safe now", said the owner, taking the black gloves off one at a time.

From a dull grey to a light pink, the matter returns to its equilibrium, at peace with its surroundings once more.

Its owner leans over a granite balustrade looking out on an alien world. From a golden mansion high up on a black mountainside, the owner can see the scorched red earth with fast flowing lava moving in rivers of fire in every direction, like a large orange spider web of chaos. The sky is a deep purple filled with green incandescent clouds that rain acid.

Nothing lives here anymore. Nothing truly alive anyway.

"And to think we were so close to losing this future...my child", hissed *Master Joe* to the now sedated brain floating in its preserved liquid, unaware of its fate and unable to respond.

•

Reading this ridiculous revelation, the renegade readers recklessly ruined the respectful and rational ending, turning it into a reprehensible and repugnant reincarnation of its once righteous self. Remorseful for their rebellious and regretful ways, the readers repent to the rugged and ravishing rhyming narrator who reserves his right to seek a radical retribution.

Let that be a lesson to you!

What the hell was that anyway?

Was it all a dream? A computer simulation? A bad case of food poisoning? Is that Joe's brain in the jar and if so, when did *Master Joe* get it and how?

I bet you are thinking this is a great setup for a sequel, a little cliff-hanger to keep you wanting more, a teaser to tantalize your novelist taste buds, a capitalist strategy to bleed you of your hard-earned money?

It breaks my non-existent heart to tell you the answer is no. That's all the information I have. My omnipresent hands are tied.

Sure, you can re-read this glorified toilet roll of a book to look for clues but I'm out of here. I have other tall tales to tell, mediocre myths to mangle and overall crappy storylines to polish into shining turds of truth for the masses.

Feel free to follow me on more fantastical adventures that make children cry and publishers want to die, because let's face it, your life is meaningless and you have nothing better to do!

To those who followed my instructions at the beginning and enjoyed the ride, thank you and goodnight.